Demitasse Divorce

by

Richard Cirulli

CCB Publishing
British Columbia, Canada

Demitasse Divorce

Copyright ©2019, 2021 by Richard Cirulli
ISBN-13   978-1-77143-411-9
First Edition, Revised

Library and Archives Canada Cataloguing in Publication
Title: Demitasse divorce / by Richard Cirulli.
Names: Cirulli, Richard, 1952-, author
Identifiers: Canadiana (print) 20190230894 | Canadiana (ebook) 20190230878 |
ISBN 9781771434119 (softcover) | ISBN 9781771434126 (PDF)
Classification: LCC PS3603.I78 D46 2019 | DDC 813/.6—dc23

Note: All poems contained herein were written by Richard Cirulli, unless otherwise credited to the poem's author.

Cover artwork credit: SelfPubBookCovers.com/Island

Interior artwork credit: Cupid and Psyche © Nastasic | iStockPhoto.com

Publisher: CCB Publishing
             British Columbia, Canada
             www.ccbpublishing.com

"Falling in love is a cruel game
we call happiness."

Richard Cirulli

Dedication

To John Fatula my college English professor...
the magician... who turned an aspiring architect into
a writer, poet, and playwright

Thank You

A special thanks to my good friend and editor Patricia L. Casey for all her dedication and commitment that made this revised edition possible. And for enduring all of my existential and gnostic brain eruptions over the past two decades.

Of Note

Fiction is merely non-fiction penned nom de plume.

Contents

Preface

The Last Bonhomme

October's cold winds
Arrived early and unannounced
Disguised as a jester's smile
Stripping the trees of their rainbow blaze
Denying my eyes of autumn's delight

Orphaned leaves lined my reflective path
Counting them as all my year's past

Now standing naked and tall
Twisted by time
Like a bare tree in the wind
Ready to embrace
The winter of my life

October's cold chill
Whispered her sacred shibboleths
Into my searching soul
Telling me
All the bonhommes have gone home

With autumn's blaze now under foot
And the light of day
Now painted grey
The sun will now shine
Only on xeric days

I was awoken from my reverie
By winter's first snow
That covered the gardens
Where flowers once bloomed

The streets were full of empty faces
Hurrying with no place to go
Making slush everywhere they go
Yes
All the bonhommes have gone home

Existentially Elia

Homo homini lupus
(Man is a wolf to man)

We humans love expressions and clichés. They are shortcuts of sorts, used to bypass critical thinking and to deny ourselves the truth. They replace free thought, possibly avoid disappointment, and allow us to believe talk is cheap. They result in outcomes one rarely can afford because they bankrupt us morally and emotionally.

Clichés, expressions, labels, they allow us to place our thoughts into self-constructed little boxes that shelter us from our fear of ourselves and our self-disappointments. We consume them like a child does candy – sweet to the tongue, bitter to the bones.

Clichés are like adjectives, small words with broad bandwidths of meaning, never quantitative, used subjectively to fit one's twisted agenda.

People are addicted to labels – for themselves and others – often using them wrongly to slander the innocent, placate their insecurities, and raise the ire of their intended victims. Most labels are based on contorted opinions, rarely on facts. If the facts contest or render a misguided label as wrong, the addict continues to lie to himself, seeking validation from anyone who will embrace the lie; like a fly seeking dung.

Labels, clichés, expressions are the head food of the mentally lazy; those too emotionally feeble to ask why and who never admit to a wrong or transgression. Rather, they reduce truth to subjective rhetoric and make their opinions fact via a persuasive tongue spoken to the profane whose consensus they seek. They make easy converts out of fools by evangelizing miscreant dialogues to satisfy their ignorance.

I have a passionate disdain for clichés and labels. I avoid them at all costs. I am far too much of a free thinker – an existentialist – to box myself into the small confines of such pigeonholes.

One would think that with time and age, people might mature and grow out of their self-imposed ignorance and dismiss the lies. Well, most don't! They continue to banter within their primitive minds, successfully turning their lies into redefined definitions of truth.

My thoughts had strayed from the divorce papers that lay in front of me. I am going over them one last time, preparing to sign and present them to my wife. My mind wanders with uncontrollable thoughts and past memories that ring within my head and haunt me like will-o'-wisps. I am about to toss the unsigned divorce papers into my cache when I become distracted with thoughts of my marriage, children, career, and all the open conflicts of my life that have either rendered pain or happiness. At what cost? What sacrifice? I pull out my journal and script a question. No, maybe a goal. A quest? I just don't know.

What is my raison d'être?

In middle age that is a difficult thought to navigate, challenging and humbling. I am turning two-score-plus, beginning to feel old and thinking that if I make it to three-score I will look back on today as part of my younger days. We become more doubtful, more confident in our frailties and uncertainties as we age. A life change for sure. I am beginning to believe that in middle age we do have fewer options. Our mortal time is finite, complete with an unknown expiration date. Wisdom teaches us to be prudent in life, to never live the life of a fool. Oh yes, those fucking clichés; save them for a rainy day.

How many peoples' paths have we crossed who worked hard, scrimped and saved, squirreling away their money for their later years, which never arrived? Their justification being that the fool who forsakes the unknown tomorrow wages his bet on the reality of the moment. They know all too well the past is a land we can never return to, and the future is just a dream that has not yet arrived. In hindsight, the mortar that bonds the foundation of our mortality is also the lime that weakens the cement of our footings when we face life's enigmas.

Should one pass up the tempting flesh of infidelity for the sake of morality and fear a life of regrets, all the while finding comfort in knowing you had done right? This only offers a false compromise and an illusion found in hindsight when one finds your spouse is not playing the marriage game by the same rules. The moralist who also is a realist knows lies coexist with truth. This is the reality of the matter. As children we are taught to tell the truth and admonished not to lie. Though we are never taught how to lie, it comes quite naturally. Lying is like defecating; we don't need an owner's manual to know what to do.

I continue on with my existential brain virus as I turn the pages of my divorce papers for another "last" review. Now it is only a matter of time and money.

Divorces are never easy, even if amicable. It's not just a matter of lost love. Love I place in the category of single-word clichés. Love is merely a vocal utterance spoken at a time of physical passion and animal emotion. It is rarely the spoken expression of a spiritual bond seeking a higher order of the sensual flesh – though maybe for a while until age or temptation inserts itself. With utterances from a tongue unattached to the soul and using a broadband of definitions, we change the rules with capriciousness and believe that penalties are levied only if we are caught. "What they don't know won't hurt them," is one of those dreaded clichés, spoken by those with little conscience and an arrogance that lets them believe they will never be found out. And, of course, never forgetful of their lust for another cliché, "what's good for the goose is good for the gander," they say. "No one likes a taste of their own medicine."

Clichés!

Legally, divorces are never on time, always lagging behind the emotional end rendered within your soul that tells you, you must go. That silent voice is always on time whether you believe it or not. Yet you stay, held back by those dammed fucking clichés. "Stay married for the children," and yes, of course, the oath of marriage itself sworn before the altar with everyone you call friends and family in attendance. "For better or for worse."

Clichés!

Yes, I believe I am a moral man who paid a king's ransom in money, sweat, time and honor, only to be rendered a fool by her infidelity. O yes, for better or worse! What is the wise and forgiving man's reward? We can't preempt such behaviors. At best all one can do is decide how to respond to an unwarranted transgression. What are the options, and what is the real solution? If I forgive with an act of compassion, would it be returned if I engage in the same transgression? Would my forgiveness and understanding end her illicit love affair? Would she just assume I am too caring to be taken seriously and continue on, turning my understanding and forgiveness into a sign of weakness? Do two wrongs make a right? No, but it begs the question: Should a spouse be a teacher and a judge?

The opportunity costs of marriage are very high, for its debt of lost time with the wrong person can never be purchased at any price. Maturity teaches us that an appetizer of the flesh renders us crumbs for the main course, leaving us with an unfulfilled appetite for desserts.

My interior philosophical conundrum is broken when Karen, one of the café owners, comes by with my second cup of demitasse.

Karen and her husband opened the Demitasse Café about a year ago. I believe they were a bit risk oblivious when they invested in their café, being one of the first establishments on Main Street to start the gentrification of the village. The Demitasse Café replaced the greasy spoon coffee shop with upscale coffee complete with alfresco seating and white tablecloths fitted out with fresh flowers. The interior is decorated with rustic woodworking, painted in pastel colors along with bookcases filled with hardcover classics. The storefront is equally inviting with true divided light wood windows.

The café is located at the end of Main Street, just over the tracks from the quaint train station, and offers a placid view of the Hudson River and Storm King Mountain. The village, once lost in time, is now awakened by New York City artists and antique seekers arriving daily on the train.

The village is south of the Hudson River freshwater line located about thirty miles north in Poughkeepsie. The scent of the salt water adds to the ambience and charm of the café.

I am awakened from my reverie, which vacillates between my pending divorce and my critique of the café, when Karen pours my second cup of demitasse. The break affords me the opportunity to catch a casual glance of the woman at the table next to me. Her beauty catches my eye. I am a man who appreciates the aesthetics of life.

My mind is on existential overload. I detach myself from my intellectual posturing and the legal paperwork I am procrastinating on. I find some daylight in my mental misery when I review the specifications and purchase agreement for the artist's loft that soon will be my new home. All I have to do is place my John Hancock on the bottom line and write out the check. It will be that simple. I have cancelled all my meetings for the day just to have time alone to weigh my decision and rebrand my life according to me.

Anais

I am sipping my demitasse coffee alfresco-style at my favorite haunt – a little natural foods café owned by some middle-aged hippie bohemian couple overlooking the Hudson River in Cold Spring, New York. I am caught up in my daydream of fantasies and desires. I have some time on my hands before I head into the city. The mid-October afternoon is sunny and cool, so I grabbed my camera and headed out in the hope of finding those lost missing pages from my book of life. At forty-two the pages are being turned fast by the wrinkled hands of uncompromising and cruel Father Time.

I place my cup of coffee down on the white linen tablecloth as I catch a vanity glimpse of my reflection in the café's window. "Not bad," I say to myself. "I still have it, though with a grey hair or two, no exaggerated frown lines, and my body is holding its own against time in the gravity war. But for how long?" In honest reflection I muse, "I am not lying to myself or in denial. I still see myself as a youthful and desirable woman. Can I still turn a man's gaze in my direction?"

My fleeting beauty pales, compromised by the ugliness of my aged and unfulfilled desires. I have become a prisoner of my own choices and conventions, and motherhood. I could attempt to outrun Father Time who never plays fair, stealing one's youth with impunity all the while knowing our finite time comes without a known expiration date. I can no longer pass my days wishing or fantasizing about my unfulfilled life. Self-inflicted sacrifices are the most painful to bear. We are all forced to balance our morality against our desires. It is always a zero-sum game of winner takes all. There is no consolation prize for the looser, and the odds increase against us with each new day.

My vanity gaze is interrupted by a man entering the café. He is greeted by name by the waitress who flashes a wide smile as she escorts him to the table next to me. The waitress soon reappears with a cup of demitasse without him ever uttering his menu choice. He looks 40-ish, I would guess. He has a hybrid look about him, one you just can't place in a box. He wears a devilish smirk, though his smile is as innocent as a little boy's. He is as confident as he is aloof, a contradiction true to himself. He is wearing a blue pinstripe suit and polished shoes. His hair is dark and thick, worn longer than typical business convention would appreciate. His movements are fluid, though his eyes are rigid, indicating he is engaged in some type of cerebral analytical thought. He appears oblivious to his surroundings, though in reality he is in complete control. Is he a gentleman or a rogue?

"Odd," I think to myself, "I have been a frequent customer here, but I have never encountered him before. He's known on a first-name basis, appears to be well-liked. Is he a good tipper or maybe just a flirt and a ladies' man?"

As he sips his demitasse, he writes some notes on a legal pad intermittently between what appear to be sketches. He is in deep thought, distant and removed from his surroundings, lost in his work, or so I think. I take this opportunity to study him more closely. He makes me curious. "Who is he and what is his story?"

As I fix my gaze upon him, I momentarily lose consciousness of my surroundings, forsaking the social grace to not stare. I thought he was so engrossed in his doodling and thinking that he would not take notice. He catches my stare in the reflection on the window and raises his head to catch me off guard with a disarming smile.

The dance has begun.

I smile back and cross my legs exposing just enough flesh without being obscene or unladylike. I catch his gaze as he follows my movements with attentive eyes. Checkmate!

I watch with triumph as I see him enjoying my modest exhibition, and just smile back to affirm our mutual pleasure.

Without moving his head and with a subtle shift of his eye, he glances at my left hand. He finds no encumbrance of marriage there. Hmm, a gentleman with a silent morality, manifested by his calculated actions. Life never plays fair when one's desires are ripe. The fruits of passion either die on the vine as unlived fantasies and regrets or are lived with jest and fulfillment to be picked with reckless abandon and without inhibition from the lower limbs of our rogue emotions.

Refills

The man turns to face me and breaks the stalemate by inquiring if I am a photographer, adding "it's a great autumn day to capture the natural beauty of the Hudson Valley. Will I make a poor first impression if I ask your name"?

I respond, "It's Anais, and no, you make a rather gentlemanly first impression Elia."

He pauses for a moment, then inquires, "Do you know me? Have we met before"?

"No this is our first encounter. I heard the waitress greet and address you by name. You must be a frequent customer, or you're just very popular."

"The former," he replies, "I stop here every morning for coffee on my way to my office in Westchester."

I continue to gaze at him with an impish smile and twirl my hair with flirtatious intent. If he is a seasoned lover, he will easily pick up on my suggestive body language.

He continues on to make conversation. "Anais, a very interesting name. I believe it is derived from the name of the Persian goddess of water and love, Anahita."

He further inquires, "And, what is your last name?"

"Bonheur" I reply.

He begins to loosen up a bit, and then responds, "It's a French/ Belgium name, Walloon I believe."

I am quite impressed with his knowledge and how he has picked up on my ethnicity. I use his response as a gateway to move closer to his character.

"Humph, I see you are quite knowledgeable. Yes, I am of

Walloon ancestry though removed from it by a few generations. How do you know this? With a name like Elia, you must be Italian, correct? So how do you know so much about my Walloon heritage?"

"I am just well read," he replies.

Are you an academic?" I ask.

"For now, let's just say I am an artist."

"You are a bit evasive," I say.

Elia retorts, "No, just not vain and arrogant."

I continue to be his muse. "Elia, Italian right?"

"Yes Anais, and one generation removed."

He then takes the initiative, or more to the point, the bait.

"Anais, please join me at my table if you'd like to continue our conversation. Would you like another demitasse?"

I oblige with a knee-jerk reaction. "Karen, please bring us another round of demitasse."

I was hoping he would ask me, though he caught me off guard. I was planning to play a little hard to get. No pain, no gain.

"Anais, please let me first get all of my papers out of our way. They are distracting."

"They look rather important and legal. Are you sure you have time to talk? We can pick up the conversation another time."

"Anais, that won't be necessary. And yes, there are some pressing legal documents here, paperwork from my attorney, specifically the purchase agreement for an artist's loft I am planning to buy."

Elia has piqued my interest and my libido as well. "So, you are an artist for real. A photographer? You were quick to pick up on my camera."

"Anais, I am just an artist of life."

So, Elia, where is this loft? Are you moving out of the area into the city?"

His eyes light up as he more intensely focuses on our conversation. I am feeling confident. I still have it. It is clear we have a mutual interest in each other. I now focus on every word, pause, and inflection.

Elia looks into my eyes. "Anais, heavens no, I love the Hudson Valley. I found a great deal on a first offering for an artist's loft on the Hudson. It's the top floor with a majestic view."

"Elia, it sounds magnificent. You must be a romantic at heart."

"Yes Anais, guilty as charged. It is a fate I must now embrace."

"Why Elia, are you telling me you can control your fate and destiny?"

"Well, today I can with just a few pen strokes," he says.

"Anais, tell me more about yourself," he continues. "What life stories would you like to share? You look like an interesting woman. Am I being too inquisitive? I should warn you that I am a curious intellectual and conversationalist. Please tell me more about your photography."

"To be truthful Elia, I just dabble in it. I use it as my mental health break. You know, to get away from the home and my three teenage daughters for the day. I need some time to myself and to develop my self-interests. I want to reinvent myself before I become obsolete."

"I truly understand Anais. Are you married? I am a traditionalist and would never trespass on another man's turf. In principle I am not a poacher."

"A gentleman with principles, such a rarity today. The moniker is symbolic of a mundane life, or perhaps a fool.

Integrity has its shortcomings Elia."

"Such as, Anais?"

"Regrets and lost love. So, Elia are you married? Do you have children?"

Elia hesitates for a moment, glances at the papers, and clutching his pen makes a few pen strokes.

"I am recently divorced, with two teenage girls."

"Elia, excuse my prying, but what was the reason for your divorce? How long was it in the works?"

"Anais, it would be fair to say it ran its course, we grew apart. I had married out of my class, for love is truly blind. Of course, there was the lack of spontaneity and romance. I had not taken a vow of celibacy at the altar. Please excuse me Anais, I believe I have shared far too much."

"I understand Elia, we have so much in common. I had to deal with the same issues. To be alone in a marriage is a sin, especially if you don't have to be. I came to the conclusion it was my choice, not my fate."

"Well Anais, it's a beautiful autumn day, would you be interested in a commission to photograph some of the buildings I designed in the area for my portfolio? It needs to be updated for sure."

"Elia! So, you are an architect? I would love to, but not today. I will have to take a rain check. How does Friday afternoon work? We can meet here for coffee and then spend the afternoon capturing your artwork. How does that work for you?"

"Well, it's a date. You may need to plan for a long day, we have a lot of geography to cover."

"No problem Elia, the girls will be spending time with their dad this weekend."

Anais waves off the third refill as Karen comes by with the coffee pot.

"O Elia, I am sorry. I lost track of the time. I have to drive into the city for my acting class, and then an evening audition."

"My lucky day Anais. So, you're an actress as well? Lots of luck on the audition. Can you share with me what part you are auditioning for?"

With a bit of hesitation Anais responds.

"Well, I'd rather not say, you know, in case I don't get the role. Roles are harder to come by as we age, especially for women. We are forced to push our comfort zones and take on new characters. That's the sad reality. It's a bit like marriage, the honeymoon does not last long."

Anais grabs her purse and pulls out her business card.

"Here is my business card. For business purposes, I use my married name, Travato. My ex-husband, Ben Travato, is a successful businessman in the entertainment industry. Do you know of him or of his firm?"

"No Anais, I am distant from the entertainment community, though I am sure it's an exciting business to be in."

"Yes, it's quite an exciting business, and this is what drew me towards Ben, he owns a production company and knows a lot of people in the industry. Why he still pulls a few strings for me. Ben was the one who set up this evening's audition."

"So, Anais, how could someone in the entertainment world like Ben be so unromantic and not spontaneous?

"O Elia, Ben is so much of a Svengali and businessman, not an artist at heart. You know the type. We are true artists, you and I, we share the same dreams and passions and aspire to the same desires. Why should we choose to be alone?"

Elia quickly pays the tab, along with a generous tip. He walks Anais to her car.

"Here is my business card, call me if you need to reschedule."

Anais takes the card and looks it over.

"See you Friday Elia.... Baldesarre? Did I say it right?"

Anais gets into her SUV and drives off, leaving Elia with a smile and a wave.

Just an Innocent Bystander

"Hell is other people."
–Jean-Paul Sartre

Anais left me with an oeillade as she drove away. A most fortuitous event for sure, or was it just synchronicity at work? I elected not to engage this philosophical debate within my head, but rather embraced the essence of the moment. In my unexpected romantic high, I now felt confident of my decision — one I had procrastinated on for a number of years. My signature just confirmed my emotions – "for better or for worse."

Clichés!

I turn on the radio and redline my way down to my office in Westchester. Within my reverie - more like a sexual fantasy - I am oblivious to time and space. Tom Petty's "Running Down a Dream," is playing on the radio. "So apropos," I think. "Or is it just synchronicity?"

My high flounders as I find myself driving past the home of a former client. It is a large house addition/renovation I had designed in the not-too-distant past for a former friend and business associate. The business relationship had gone south. My mind quickly turns from a positive high to a low as I find myself revisiting the events that had led to a con fuoco confrontation and break.

I had received a call from the owner, a specialty contractor with offices in the same building as my architectural practice. We had never done business before, but I had referred his company to some of my clients. He was a young Turk, a college graduate from South Carolina. He was very articulate, well mannered, and impeccably dressed – real GQ cover material. By the time he was thirty he was running his own successful and expanding commercial construction company. I was eager to assist anyone attempting to enter the gauntlet of the construction business.

Donny called me one day and asked me to meet him and his wife at a house he had recently purchased for his growing family. He had picked up a distressed property and was planning to gut it and turn it into an upscale home fit for the zip code he had just moved into. I would be meeting his wife for the first time.

When I arrived at the house, Donny and his wife were waiting out front. They made a perfect couple. His wife, Alexandra, was a tall, stunning Nordic blond. She looked radiant, with star quality.

After the introduction we walked the property as I listened to their design expectations. The work would require adding on a sizeable addition to accommodate a large master bedroom suite complete with Jacuzzi, his and her bathrooms, and a large second-floor deck to capture the surrounding views.

As I was taking notes, Donny excused himself to make a few calls. Alone with Alexandra I became uncomfortable as she walked me to the area that would be converted to the master bedroom suite. She asked me where the Jacuzzi should go.

"This space will be so romantic. I can easily see myself bathing in the Jacuzzi with a glass of champagne anticipating a romantic evening. Can you picture that?" She asked. "I hear you architects are true romantics and uninhibited libertines, and so much fun to be with."

She stared into me with her piercing blue eyes. "Is it true? Do you have a Jacuzzi in your office?"

With a self-effacing retort, I answered, "Now Alexandra, how can we architects be such party animals and libertines if we spend all our time drawing pictures with tee-squares and triangles, bent over a drafting table? It's more monastic than hedonistic."

I began to doddle a few sketches on canary tissue paper and turned to walk in the opposite direction when Donny entered the room.

"So, Elia, how is Alexandra's design taste? I hope you are writing down all her design ideas. I want to make sure you give her everything she wants. Money is no object for my beautiful wife."

Over the coming months Donny frequently stopped by the office to check on the drawings, finally approving them. I filed the plans with the local building department, and a permit was issued in short order. My contract was limited to design, complete with a professional courtesy discount. Since Donny was a licensed contractor, he would be his own general contractor and monitor the construction. It was an easy commission I believed, complete with good networking and more design leads to follow, or so I had thought.

About six months later, early one Friday morning, I received a call from Donny at my office. He told me the project was moving along fine and that he wanted to make a few design revisions before I certified the drawings and filed for the Certificate of Occupancy. He said he would be back from a business trip in South Carolina early in the afternoon and suggested a 4 p.m. meeting to include his wife. I agreed to meet them as requested, although I had previous plans to leave the office early that particular Friday to catch up with friends for dinner.

Around 3 p.m. Alexandra called to inform me Donny had to stay in South Carolina overnight to work on an estimate for one of his clients. Instead of cancelling, Donny said to have the meeting without him. I was very uncomfortable with the change of plans.

Alexandra then interjected, "Donny always leaves me alone. He is always away on business and I'm lonely. I don't want to spend another Friday night alone. Can we spend the evening together and try out that Jacuzzi you designed?"

Another man might have taken her up on this offer, never reflecting on the consequences and the sins. Counting his blessings, he'd say, "Don't look a gift horse in the mouth."

Those fucking cliches!

I was a bit dumbfounded. My mind stuttered in a dialogue with itself as to how to handle the situation. And the kicker was that I was debating whether or not I wanted to engage in an illicit infidelity with my friend's wife and cheat on my wife – even as I had proof that my wife was having an affair with a "friend" of the family.

What an existential mind fuck. How can I find essence, even when it is thrown in my lap, knowing two wrongs don't make a right? My only consolation was that I once again took the moral high ground, passing up a moment of ecstasy. Am I a moralist or a fool? Can a moralist ever truly find an essence of life without harming another?

"Elia, are you still on the phone? Did you hang up? Talk to me!" Alexandra had pleaded as I made my decision.

I had kept my voice steady despite her apparent agitation. "Sorry Alexandra," I said. "I was just multi-tasking and not doing a good job at it as you can see. Could we reschedule the meeting until next week? I generally do not schedule late Friday afternoon appointments and would like to head out early to take care of some pressing family matters. Besides, it would be better if Donny were present to agree to the design changes, to avoid meeting twice. Because we are friends and business associates,

I'm not charging for my field visits as a show of good faith."

There was a moment of silence, then Alexandra started to shout, "Well then, if that's how you feel, I take it as an insult. Good-bye Elia!" and she slammed down the phone.

About fifteen minutes later I received a screaming call from Donny telling me I had disrespected his wife, and he was going to sue me for breach of contract for not showing up. I was wise enough to know that truth would offer no defense and my morality did not serve me well. As promised, a few weeks later, I was served a summons to appear in court for breach of contract. It was my first lawsuit, initiated by a friend I was trying to protect.

"Ignorance is bliss" – just another cliché.

I am not sure, why I am dwelling on this memory with such detail, especially after coming down from the high of meeting Anais. I do laugh out loud though as I recall the final outcome of that episode. About nine months after that fateful Friday afternoon, Donny's wife gave birth to a baby boy, compliments of Donny's esteemed brother.

"Karma is a bitch." I will take exception from my disdain for those fucking cliches in this case.

I am still not sure why I am thinking about Donny and Alexandra and the cost I had paid for adhering to my prohibition against being a romantic poacher preying on frail and broken emotions and hearts.

I try to recall my conversation with Anais. She is divorced from a Svengali of a husband, with three teenage daughters to raise. We seem to be living parallel lives. All I have to do is turn those parallel lines into two vectors converging on the same target.

As I enter the architecture studio, my office manager Liz, a striking blond about my age, who I have known since high school, has checks ready for my signature. I then go to my private office and work on plans for an addition to Saint Dymphna's hospital, intentionally losing track of the time as an excuse to work late into the evening. I am avoiding going home. My house is merely a collage of bricks and sticks, a shuttered façade that hides its dark interior soul.

Around midnight, I begin thinking about Anais, wondering how her audition has gone, and what would become of us over the coming weeks.

With an uncertain mood, before heading home, I decide to write in my journal.

Elia's Journal | Wednesday | October 7, 1992 | 12:20 a.m.

A Distant Love
Scorn will follow the man
Who falls for a distant love
Even a wise man becomes her fool
For there is no greater curse
Than a love afar

Her name you certainly know
But dare not whisper
Her smile you dare to follow
As her bright eyes keep their vigil
A distant pose she denies you

She reaches into your soul
Till it is no longer yours
She injects it with intimacy that's not fair
For you cannot touch her
Though you feel her everywhere
She exists...you know
She has told you so

The Audition

It is well past midnight as I head north from Manhattan after my late-night audition. Driving on autopilot, I am experiencing an emotional overload as I reflect on the events of the day. On the one hand I am happy and curious thinking about Elia. On the other, I am not sure how the audition had gone, or if I'd get the part, even with Ben's influence. I am confused, not sure about a role that will push me into new acting genres.

At forty-plus, this would be my first nude/love scene for an indie movie and a last-chance power grab for some level of stardom and commercial visibility. I had felt at ease with Morgan, the female director, who added a soft touch and feel to the audition. But I am not sure about breaking personal taboos.

Am I acting out a fantasy I had long harbored under the convention of marriage and parenthood?

No, and I can't hold back the smirk, this is merely the first item to be crossed off my bucket list.

My body is still tingling with sexual energy. I had enjoyed it.

Should I feel guilty?

Ben had made it his point to be there, though he had never informed me. Not only is he a real Svengali, he's into voyeurism. As Ben matured, he seemed to get-off watching sex more than performing it. And he seemed to enjoy the audition more than I did, but I segregated my feelings from my acting. I would never tip my hand.

I've never been satisfied with Ben's emotionless, hard, arbitrary and capricious sexuality. I never know what to expect from him. We never connect on a spiritual or emotional level.

His hands and touch are always hard and course, even more callous than his character.

Tonight had been different. I'd felt a physical and emotional connection with Morgan.

As actors, what we stage is never reality, only a reflection of someone else's emotions and actions. Maybe we are just imitators. If I play the role of a criminal, am I really a closet criminal? Was it just good acting during my audition or was it a hidden me finally exposing myself? Will I accept that, and at what cost? Am I really a libertine at heart with my desires usurped by conventions and traditions?

I awake from my reverie somewhere on Route 9 not too far from home. The roads are empty except for a police car in the median looking to nab some early morning speeders or DWIs to make his quota.

My senses remain on overload as I continue to contemplate the day. It is as if the rest of my life's happiness hinges on it. Lost between expectation and uncertainty, I find myself dwelling on my upcoming birthday.

I'm approaching two-score, plus twenty-four months. I know I'm in denial, I refuse to think in years. I have been an emotional masochist punishing my mind with glee about approaching the perimeter of middle age.

Who determines this? Is it like when you become a major at age twenty–one and can sign contracts, take out loans, and buy alcohol? Are all twenty-one-year-olds ready emotionally to take on legal responsibilities? Hell, how many people do I know well into their later years, who still lack any level of emotional intelligence? Why don't they give tests before they issue the majority card?

I keep my focus on the road, my agitation is rising.

If twenty-one is a number, then who decides the metric for

middle age? Is it a universal biological constant? Some experts say middle-age begins at forty. Hell, if that's true I'm already over the hill.

My body is well-formed and tight. I look better than some twenty-somethings I know. No, those experts who say middle-age begins at forty-five, they are the real authorities. That gives me three more years to navigate my transition without regrets.

I am filled with so much doubt and anticipation about who I am.

The boundaries of my marriage to Ben were always fluid and contentious – and I never fully embraced motherhood. We had engaged in sexual procreation for the sake of parenthood, regardless of knowing how poorly we would fail at it. We procreated just to fit in with the rest of the "monkey see, monkey do" suburban ethos. At least we were honest enough to admit we had selfish and opportunistic tendencies. We used whatever assets, personal or financial, at our disposal to secure our epicurean desires. It's not that we didn't love our children, we just never made it a priority to show our love and affection. And the girls knew this. For every step we distanced ourselves from our daughters they took two more steps back.

Ben and I always cherished the comments we received from friends, neighbors, and teachers about how beautiful, smart, well behaved, and independent our daughters are.

The beautiful part came easy, and we can take credit for at least that. Both Ben and I have an abundance of beautiful genes. We just can't take credit for the rest of our daughters' good traits.

Well after all, what should be expected of us, we are just mere mortals. I give little to no thought to an afterlife. I am a sensual person always seeking the aesthetics of life. I make the best of what life has dealt me. I did not blueprint my life – it was pre-drawn and handed to me. I just build upon it like a master builder. This is why I am drawn to Elia. In my eyes he is a master builder. One who can reconstruct a virgin pasture into a livable habitat of geometric proportion or bring new life to an abandoned and dead building.

My mind and emotions are fulgurant as I experience my beingness rapidly decline – all brought on by what I believe is my fast-approaching menopause. I had to fabricate this lie and believe it to give myself the power to break away from my sexual alienation. Menopause, children, middle age – they are the three ugly venomous heads of the hydra ready to strike me in my moment of vulnerability.

At times my marriage has no boundaries. Ben and I are not wired to play by the rules. The only rule we seem to obey is to allow ourselves to break the rules – and we do this with capricious and arbitrary recklessness. Even with such latitude, our life together is just mediocre. We survive as two parents co-habitating together for the sake of convention and financial stability. In essence, we are each other's whore and pimp.

As I turn onto Cherry Lane, my mind fills with a myriad of wicked thoughts. I wonder how many conventional married women with children share the same thoughts, tormenting themselves with fear and shame at the prospect of ever living them out. My goal now is to live a life that exceeds all my fantasies. My bucket list is not going to include a journal of sexual regrets and lost opportunities.

As I pull into my driveway, I sigh with a deep breath, and think of Elia. Will he break my sexual isolation and offer a soft touch?

"Nothing ventured, nothing gained."

As expect, the house was dark and empty. It is rare to find all of us at the house at the same time. Upon entering, I drop my bag and the bundles of stuff from the day's errands. I go upstairs to the bedroom suite, fill the tub and add bath salts. I disrobe and take a critical look at my naked body.

Not bad for my age. I'm still in good form. I wonder how the camera captured me. What will Elia think? Fresh out of a divorce, will he be the aggressor and seduce me? Or will he be slow and insecure to act?

I know Elia with all his charisma, charm, and wit, is totally sincere. He is a gentleman who is opposed to the tack he must take to seduce me, for he is rational, in control, and principled. Elia will not breach the gentleman's line of honor, no matter how much he desires me.

It is best I play the role of the Siren – the ultimate male fantasy – and now mine as well. I will offer Elia a total release from his moral limitations. I will not take him to a world where women are not too timid to project a Siren's image, I will take charge of his male libido by being his fantasy. I am too sexually charged to play it any other way. I will lead the path and seduce him when I know he is feeling comfortable and confident.

I burn some incense as I slip into the tub, say a little prayer – a mantra – even agnostics do this occasionally in time of doubt and need. I slump back listening to my meditation music as I place my hand between my legs to engage my fantasy of Elia.

The River

I had signed the divorce papers, thanks to Anais' modest display. Well, "when the student is ready, the master arrives." Another fucking cliché! Had I fallen into an existential tailspin only to land upon a sword of profane clichés? How nauseating. It is time to take things to the next level – no more idle talk. Before I venture further with ending my marriage and engaging in a new relationship with Anais, I need some time for meditation and self-reflection.

I drive to Cold Spring, park my car and walk to my favorite bench in the park along the banks of the Hudson River, just across from the Demitasse Café. It is a shady spot – one I have visited often when I need time to contemplate a decision or take a new direction in life.

As I sit, I jot down a few comments and go through the divorce papers again, along with the purchase agreement for the loft. I think about calling my attorney, Richard Certiorari, one more time to get some direction, but catch myself. Rit is a good friend and has stopped returning my calls, tired of my procrastination and indecision.

I just sit for a while staring into the water, letting my thoughts wander as they always do when I come to sit by the river.

I don't know how much time has passed when I awake from one of my all too frequent existential reveries and begin to write in my journal. Along with the many poems that write themselves during my deep ponderings, it is where I record my thoughts for the purpose of self-analysis.

My conscience and sub conscience are one - a natural ability I possess that is the envy of the many therapists I have retained for assistance with my divorce. My wife's mental illness has taken its toll on me and I have attended frequent support groups, which take time away from my busy schedule and pressing deadlines.

After years of attending the groups, I realized the sessions had taught me much about the workings of my wife's illness but offered no solutions or cures. For the most part, the therapists played the role of peacekeeper rather than problem solver. I now go only for their peer reviews.

After spending a small fortune on private therapy, unbeknownst to my wife, the therapists' advice proved of little help. In essence they told me I had accepted the marriage vow for better or worse, and that if I really love my wife, I should forgive and forget about her affair. Further, I should accept her behavior until she is ready to seek help. Just another shallow, fucking cliché' dressed up in pretty words to cover an atrocity of broken trust and infidelity. A one-sided solution for sure. My feelings were never calculated into the equation.

I continue to sit and ponder the river. I never feel alone in its company. For me, the river is a holy and mystical place. The waters[1] speak to me in some unknown angelic Enochian[1] tongue with a soothing whispering voice alien to my ears, although I easily understand it in my soul.

Over the past several months I have spent more time in the village – in the company of the river, walking its shore in an almost catatonic state. I have neglected my practice and alienated friends. Over time the village has become a crutch for

---

[1]"The language of angels."

me as I dally about quaint book shops, looking for rare and esoteric tomes, and devouring volumes on existentialism. I eventually joined a Masonic lodge in the village in the hope it might quench my voracious appetite for a deeper spiritualism and intellectualism. For me these are the working tools of the master builder in search of his soul. I seek my higher self. I am consumed with the conflict between my flesh and my soul, like an errant knight in search of the Holy Grail.

Elia's Journal | Thursday | October 8, 1992 | 9:35 a.m.

She stood upon the river's pastoral shore
Draped within its sacred waters
Reflecting her beauty
Into its pristine tide

Her silence muted autumn's full bloom
Cascading their bright leaves
Along her path

A sweet October breeze
Teased her hair
Casting it wanton across her face
I imagined she was there

Elia's Rewind

*"Love always heals the wounded heart,
while piercing the center of your soul."*

For me to be able to move forward with my decision, I must be in a state of beingness, outside my beingness. I must end this monologue in my head and turn it into a dialogue between my emotions and logic. I can no longer intellectualize it. Since I can be brutally honest with myself, and with more clarity than the best friend or therapist can offer, I know I have to make the decision on my own. True friends will place a friendship before truth. I respect this, so I burden them not with deep questions to force them to render what they perceive to be hurtful commentary and instead will call them for a round of celebratory drinks after the fact.

I am beginning to believe even friends are merely human clichés.

My cerebral thinking is making me existentially exhausted, and to a degree distant from the overdue decisions I have to make. My mind drifts back more than twenty years to one of my first encounters with Beth, an incident that had raised a red flag of sorts. Easily said in hindsight, but to be honest with myself, I should have paid more attention to my gut feelings at the time.

It was May of 1971, and we were in our senior year of high school. We had been dating for about six months in an undefined steady relationship. Beth had just turned eighteen and was now old enough to drink legally. I took her to one of my favorite haunts, The Square Tavern, to celebrate her rite of passage.

Beth and I were on a collision course from day one, having

grown up on different sides of the same town in mid-Westchester that was divided by a white collar/ blue collar line – one of many such boundaries. Beth lived on the other side of town amidst warehouses, factories, and corner delis. That line would play out twenty years later in class warfare and now my pending divorce.

The tavern was located at the crossroads of the town's race line. Entering and exiting the bar through the front door was never problematic for us peace-loving long-hair types. The back door was a no man's land in the evening, representing the state of racial tension plaguing the nation at the time. The bar's rear parking lot was a flash point easily ignited if a white or black crossed the invisible race line that ran past the bar's rear door – a boundary respected by all for the sake of practicality, common sense, and one's physical well-being.

I frequented the tavern often with my friends. It was our hangout of sorts. My friends and Beth's friends did not gel. It was rare if we ever partied together. We could never dance the same dance.

On that night Beth was dressed in the fashion of the day – a bit provocative – but the times they were a changing. She had a good slim and proportioned body – hot is a better description - standing at 5'-4" with long shapely legs that were a perfect match for her hot pants and high-heeled shoes. Her low-cut tank top revealed enough cleavage to excite and arouse my bursting hormones. She had long brown hair that reached below her shoulders, which she often wore up in a barrette. Her eyes were crystal-clear blue and her skin porcelain white. Her skin she inherited from her mother's Polish genes, her dark brown hair and blue eyes from her Sicilian father, one generation removed.

Beth and I found easy seating at the bar. It was early on a Friday evening and the regular crowd had not yet arrived. I ordered Beth her drink of choice, a white wine, and ordered myself a glass of Southern Comfort. I made a toast to her having reached the legal drinking age, and then we hugged and kissed. I told Beth I was expecting some friends to join us for her birthday celebration, friends she would be meeting for the first time.

By the time we ordered our second round, the bar was starting to get crowded, and I noticed a few of my friends across the room checking out the band – a rather bad cover band, more wannabe than talent. Beth was now feeling the effects of the wine and was becoming a bit affectionate. Up until now she had limited my sexual advances to kissing and feeling her up. Beth then ordered a third round for herself. Her glass was half full when she turned to me and removed the barrette that was holding her long hair up in a bun of sorts. As I approached her, she pushed me away and shook her head to let her hair fall upon her bare shoulders. She gave me a contentious look, pushed me aside, and walked down the bar to where a man was sitting having a drink. He had a tough looking face and bulging biceps. His voice was gravely as he ordered his next shot of Scotch.

Beth nuzzled up beside him. "Hey what's your name? I'm Beth. Will you buy me a drink?"

"My name is John, and this is not a cool idea," he responded. "It would be an insult to your boyfriend."

Beth was taken aback. "He's not my boyfriend. Why he is only a guy friend I hang out with. What's the big deal anyway?"

John pushed her aside. "Beth this is not the way to treat a friend.

Beth quickly retorted, believing she was being insulted, "So you won't buy me a drink."

If you don't respect your friendship with Elia, I will. You should do your poaching elsewhere."

"What are you talking about John? How do you know his

name?"

"Beth, Elia is my best friend, he invited me here to celebrate your birthday."

As I walked over to join them, John pulled me over to his side. "Hey Elia, let's get the hell out of here, and let Beth go trawling at the bar. There's a live band playing tonight at the Beachcomber in Rye, the next town over. I will go pick up Diane and you can meet me there. My sister will be there as well. She has an eye for you. I'll meet you there at 6:30. I'll also pick up your bar tab."

Beth ran back to the other side of the bar and ordered another drink for herself. She turned her back on me and sulked.

John and I rendezvoused at the Beachcomber, along with Diane and John's sister. I ordered a round of drinks, then we all headed to the dance floor to dance the night away to the beat of a real band. John's sister was quite attractive and a flirt. I only wish I could remember her name. We did a few slow dances together and took the opportunity to embrace and kiss on the dance floor. We both had our hands all over each other, taking liberties with each other's geography.

John and Diane were too engrossed in their own world to pay much heed to our public acts of social sexuality. If I recall correctly, around 9:00ish the band took a break, and Diane and John's sister headed to the ladies' room. I told John, it would be best for me to go back, find Beth and take her home. John became a bit upset with my plan.

"Hey Elia, are you fucking crazy? Why would you care about that crazy bitch who tried to publicly insult you? What would have happened if I wasn't there? Who would she have hit on, and left you there like some fool? Elia, you don't need that crazy bitch, you out class her."

I was unmoved. "John, I have to be smart, I was the one who

picked her up from her house. If she does something stupid and does not make it home tonight, the police are going to come looking for me. With long hair I'm already guilty. I'm not going to jail for that crazy bitch. You know that bar is located at the crossroads of the race line, and a few blocks from the river. If she is found floating the river, the cops are going to come after me! My DNA is all over her!"

"Fuck her! She is not worth it Elia."

"But John, I have no choice."

"You're right Elia, I can't help you. I'm going to take Diane home. What am I going to tell my sister?"

"I am sure she will understand. I'll call you if I need anything."

"Lots of luck Elia, though I think you are a righteous fool."

I remember going back to the tavern. It was around 9:30ish, and the bar was unusually quiet with few patrons. Beth was nowhere in sight. As I was about to nurse another drink to give me time to think about what I should to do next, I heard the owner scream across the bar from the kitchen.

"Hey is there a guy named Elia here. If there is, you better go to the rear parking lot NOW! Check out what's going on in the rear parking lot. There is some crazy bitch out there in some kind of big trouble. She keeps calling for some guy named Elia."

I walked over to the owner – I think his name was Vinnie – and introduced myself. He just shook his head. "Hey buddy, I don't want any trouble. Now get the fuck out of here and take care of this. You're on your own. God save you."

I left the bar through the rear entrance, entered the unlit parking lot, and crossed the race-line into no-man's land.

There I was, a long-haired peace-loving white guy, wearing bell bottoms and a white frilled shirt, standing 5'-11" tall and weighing in at about 145 pounds.

As I walked with trepidation through the deserted parking lot, except for a few parked cars, empty liquor bottles, and a few used syringes, I heard Beth crying. The sound was haunting, she was sobbing like a child. I found her sitting between a few cars with a cigarette hanging from her mouth, her make-up running down her face, and her hair in disarray. There was vomit all over her and on the pavement.

As I approached, she would not look at me. In between her sobs she kept repeating, "Elia, I am fucked up. I got problems. You don't understand. I am fucked up and useless. I am nothing but human garbage. Please don't try to help me!"

I went over to take her hand and help her up "Beth are you alright? What is going on? What happened?" I asked.

As I was about to pull her up, she puked again.

"Beth, get up and steady yourself. We have to get out of here fast! Do you understand? I am taking you home."

That's when I saw a big black man appear out of the shadows and walk down the street. I immediately sized him up. He was at most in his early twenties, a few inches shorter than me, and wearing tight jeans and an athletic tee-shirt that defined his huge biceps and barrel chest. He also sported a large well-groomed Afro. I had never seen this man before and sensed a serious confrontation.

Beth was still on the ground, on her ass, with her legs spread. The man approached looking directly at Beth.

"Hey pretty baby you want to come to daddy for some real loving? Your legs and ass look like they can use some real lovin. Let me take care of you and take you out of your misery. You ain't in no position to refuse me, and there ain't nobody who can protect you now. So, what's ya say baby?"

Beth looked up at him, "Just go fuck yourself!" she screamed.

The man then got into my face. "Hey, you skinny ass mother

fucking white boy, your bitch got no right to disrespect me, especially in my fucking neighborhood. And hey white boy, looks like you got no fight in you at all. I want you and your bitch to apologize now, or you are going to have to fight your way out of here. You got no choice man!"

I knew full well I was outclassed, and I was not a fighter. My only option was to rely on street smarts.

"Hey man, chill out. This bitch called the heat and is going to cry rape, and the bar owner told me the man is on the way. Hey man, I ain't spending no time in prison for her, and hey, with my long hair and you a black man the police are going to accuse us both of rape and drug possession. We'll be handcuffed before the night is out. This is not about disrespect, it's about survival man. I am out of here dude."

The black man looked me in the eye. "Hey man thanks for the heads up. What's your name?"

"Elia."

"Elia? I don't know what the fuck kind of name Elia is. My name is Bronson. If anyone tries to fuck with you in this neighborhood, just mention my name. No motherfucker is going to touch you."

I thanked him and gave him a joint.

As I began to walk away, Bronson called my name, "Hey Elia, here." He grabbed my hand, placed two pills in my palm, and clasped my hand closed. "Compliments of Bronson," he said.

He then ran up the street and disappeared into the shadows of darkness, just as he had appeared.

It was now well-past Beth's midnight curfew. I picked her up off the ground, walked her to my father's new Audi and placed her in the back seat. She puked again.

I dropped her off at home and watched her stagger to the front door. Once she was inside, I drove away. I was relieved I had avoided a close call at the tavern and annoyed I had been placed in harm's way due to Beth's behavior.

The house was dark when I arrived home. My father had a hot temper, and I knew the smell of puke in his new car would be a flash point. I quietly sneaked into the kitchen, loaded myself up with cleaning supplies and went back to the car to get rid of Beth's mess.

I painstakingly cleaned each nook and cranny, knowing my father was a fanatic about his car. I even cleaned the magnetic Saint Christopher statue on the dashboard and the hanging rosary beads and placed them back in their original positions. It was a real display of my father's hypocrisy in light of the open box of condoms I found under the driver's seat, along with air fresheners and mouthwash. I took the liberty to take a few condoms as a reward for cleaning his car.

I lost track of the time and fell asleep in the back seat out of genuine fatigue. Around 8:00ish I was awakened by a knock on the window.

"Hey Elia, why are you sleeping in my car? Are you fucking drunk, or high on drugs or something? Just look at your blood shot eyes. Were you out all night with some whore girlfriend in my new car? Get the fuck out of my car!"

As I exited the car, trying to pull my disheveled self together, my father grabbed me by the collar and threw me against the car. When I turned around to face him, he slapped me back hand across my face.

"Tell me Elia, why did you fall asleep in my car? Were you afraid I would find you high when you came home last night?"

"Well, if you want the truth Dad," I said. "Beth was taken ill last evening, and when I drove her home, she vomited in the back seat. I spent all evening cleaning up the mess so I could return your new Audi in good condition."

My father looked me in the eye and slapped me across my face again.

"You fuckin stupid kid, that's the price you pay for getting a blow job in a car. Hope it was worth it!"

Elia's Existential Inferno

"Lasciate ogne speranza, voi ch'intrate."
–Dante[2]

My thought regressions to the past were like journeys across the river Acheron to Hell proper, to be ferried across by Charon declaring to me, *Vuolsi cosi cola dove si puote cio che si vuole.*[3]

Why do I need to torture myself with all these reruns of the past? Do I need to do this as my motivation to file the divorce papers? Have I become so forgiving and understanding of Beth's illness, even when she is off her meds that I have rendered myself a fool, a martyr, a masochist? I know this has gone on far too long. My friends are right, I am always trying to mend Beth's broken wing in the hope she will learn to fly again. I am living in a fool's paradise. I lack nisus in my goal to achieve my self-actualization. If I just let go, I will be able to walk out of this xeric life and place myself on the summit of Maslow's hierarchy of needs.

Yes, those fucking clichés "stay married for the sake of the kids!" and that pathetic marriage oath "for better or worse!" Anais is right, loneliness is not one's fate, it is a martyr's choice. My thoughts of actually believing I can help Beth are mere delusions of my magnanimous nature. I can no more help her in her low mental state than I can raise her above her plebian world.

Sartre was right, "humanity is a useless passion."

---

[2] "Abandon all hope, ye who enter here.". Dante
[3] "It is willed there where is power to do / That which is willed." -Dante

And to what do I attribute my current sad state of affairs? Should I lament and convince myself circumstances are against me? Do I seek false solace in the novels of Zola, by convincing myself I should blame Beth's actions and behavior on heredity, environmental influences, and a class that placed her in this psychological and organic mental decline? When she is off her meds and out of control, her mantra is, "This is just the way I am. There is nothing anyone can do about it."

Beth's self-taught quietism, which she plagiarized from her social environment – her hive-mind mentality – she worships as a talisman to elude the pain of truth. With aplomb she recites the fatalist dogma, "Others can do what I can't do."

I should know better than to lament my condition and reaffirm I am nothing more than my own life project. I have no choice now but to draw my own portrait as I would like to see myself and set it before a hostile landscape which I have no control over. I must attempt this gauntlet and navigate myself to the summit of my life. My self-portrait is my free will, and the hostile landscape of life is my destiny that I am free to challenge. I should not use my morality as an excuse for not taking action.

My marriage is a plague that has spread throughout my beingness. The existentialists were correct, "existence precedes essence." This is not my mantra to recite like a nursery rhyme to put me to sleep. Rather, is it my reason to find my essence in life to wake me from my martyr's sleep. For I am a martyr without a cause. In my present state I'm evangelizing no god, only mocking God by competing with Him for attention. I stone myself believing each stone strike is a mark of honor – seeking pity from the pitiless.

I am wise enough to know I should base all my logic and actions on truth. What options are there if I truly seek to transmute my existence into an essence? I must first desecrate my old façade of delusions and acknowledge the Cartesian cogito, "I think therefore I am." This is the truth that confirms our self-awareness. If I choose to live outside this cogito, I will relegate the remainder of my life to a series of unanswered probabilities. Why should I flounder in the lowlands of doubt, when I can walk the straight and narrow path to the horizon of truth? Truth is absolute and will set you free, regardless how painful, and at times even absurd.

> *"...But to that second circle of sad hell,*
> *Where 'mid the gust, the whirlwind, and the flaw*
> *Of rain and hail-stones lovers need not tell*
> *Their sorrows, Pale were the sweet lips I saw,*
> *Pale were the lips I kiss'd and fair the form*
> *I floated with, about that melancholy storm."*
> —Dante

Anais and I have already started our mutual seduction. Was our Demitasse encounter an act of synchronicity? Only heaven knows. It was our first act of foreplay, where our senses came alive, erupting from our long-dormant Kundalini serpent power – that sexual chakra energy that makes us fantasize about our next encounter.

Friday seems like an eternity away. I am lost in fantasies of caressing her naked body in my arms and kissing her from head to toe. I want to explore her intimacies with the curiosity of an inexperienced virgin.

I lament with the caution of wisdom and maturity. Have I found my true paramour or, am I being drawn through another inferno by a Dido in disguise? Will her intimate secrets and treasures lead me in another walk through Hell?

We all are blessed with the curse of sexual desire. We are

41

never satisfied. No sooner do we end our lovemaking when desire calls us back again like an eternal echo. We are sexual animals. Like the myth of Sisyphus, we labor to push our desires and sexual exploits up the steep mountain, reaching its summit with rapture and orgasm only to have our rapture vanish below us as a thundering boulder coming to rest where we found it. Then we push it back up the face of the mountain again, motivated by our fantasies – it's our emotional foreplay.

Elia's New Kama

"Woman is the sacrificial fire,
The lips of her yoni the fuel
The hairs around them the smoke
And her love temple itself the flame.

The act of entry is the kindling
The blaze of pleasure is the sparks.
In this fire the gods offer up seed grain
Of which sacred offering, man is born."
–Mallanaga

Anais is a beautiful woman, she captivates me. There is a synchronicity at work here. She will be the touch that will push my hand to finalize my divorce. I fantasize about her often. My melancholy thoughts are transmuted into sanguine daydreams of making love to her - especially in my new loft. I am confident her sexuality is advanced and mature, unlike Beth who prefers a 15-minute romp after getting shit-faced at a bar – so typical of American sexuality. Why should anything so pleasurable be truncated to a few minutes of unconscious physical fucking? It is so barbaric.

For Beth, foreplay is a profanity. She was raised to believe sex is a sin, whose only purpose is for procreation. This most likely gave rise to her need to be intoxicated when having sex, so she would never remember having it and be alleviated from her self-imposed guilt when sobering up.

Beth finds sex obscene in her sober and even-keel states. At best she views it as a marital privilege rather than a right of adulthood – a privilege she metes out arbitrarily and conspicuously. She is unable to see sex as an intrinsic part of humanity's higher nature. She is unable to embrace its gratification and benefit as a source of happiness, health, and beauty.

I miss the days of prolonged and erotic love making denied me after my marriage to Beth. I was never a believer that sex starts in the bedroom and should be performed with much operose. Rather, I prefer that foreplay commences when spending time with a paramour at a romantic dinner at the best restaurants, with the best ambience, foods, and wine. I enjoy watching her subtle womanly moves, smiles, and graces that build anticipation for what is to come. With whispering, seductive voices we are transmuted into virgins again, seeking our first love and rite of passage.

In Anais' presence, I feel like a long-overdue virgin, waiting to be freed from my self-imposed celibacy. I am going to make my fantasies a reality again with Anais. We both need to extend the boundaries of our sexual pleasures to secure our erotic freedom and expression. We are twins sharing the womb of sexual deprivation, seeking our emancipation. Anais and I share that riotous artist's blood, which demands we seek the aesthetic of life in all our actions and thoughts, making us the true romantics and outliers we are.

I begin to plan, or maybe anticipate, how our sexual encounter will play out. Who will make the first move? Will I place my character as a gentleman before my desires and withhold outright passes? Or, with my long pent-up desires will I act too fast, and turn her off? How will she dance this minuet? Is she a cerebral chess player, or a woman with a specific agenda and expectation?

Humph, "haste makes waste" -- another dam cliché to

constrain us by tying us down to the conventions of tradition. A true romantic breaks the narrow radius of such restraint.

I cannot afford to miss out on this life event. Anais and I are both artists creating the illusions we desire within ourselves and the lovers we seek. Women do not feel desired and appreciated by men who are distracted and unresponsive. I will restrain myself from being rakish in my seduction. I will not, like some men, take advantage of a woman's weakness by being an emotional chameleon, disloyal, dishonest, and amoral. Though these seem to be the characteristics of her ex-husband, Ben, which drew her to him. I have to assume a man can stir a woman's repressed longings by adapting the rakish persona mix of danger and pleasure.

But Anais and I are older now. The dreams of our youth are simply that – dreams – either shattered or reduced to functional levels of disappointment. The weak souls – those who love to lament life more than live it – are drawn to other people's broken dreams, unconscious that these represent their life's fantasies. These broken hearts long for adventure and romance, though they fear finding it. Once their desired adventures and romance become reality, they believe they can have no more fantasies to imagine.

The absurdity of life.

If I don't play by the rules of profane seduction that society has imposed, will I be labeled a terrible 'idiot' like Meursault, the stranger, in Camus' novel? Do I need to be a rake with sweet and shallow words to seduce Anais? Maybe should I defer to Kierkegaard's maxim, "the surest way of being mute is not to hold your tongue, but to talk."

Elia's Journal | Thursday | October 9, 1992 | 5:30 a.m.

Whispers
The winds whispered memories of her
Muted name
Her fair northern skin
Was clear as the blue sky
Covering her unblemished sins.

She walked oblivious to her beauty...
Though no stranger to men
Her smile radiated the dawn
Breaking the dark night of my soul within
She hid under her umbrella of passions
She spoke from her heart with words
Never said.

She was misguided as she was true
Her affections were well read.

She danced with pennies in her eyes
To cover her golden heart
She exposed herself in her mystery
Never casting a doubt.

Sexual Preamble

Elia and Anais know the photography session is just a preamble to seduction. They are confident they want each other's sex – it is obvious how quickly their chemistries have galvanized. Caught up in their individual sexual fantasies, each succumbs to their own uncertainties by second-guessing the other's modus operandi. Anais knows Elia, fresh from a recent divorce and a less than romantic marriage, will be quick to act. Elia, on the other hand, caught up in Anais' charm and beauty, had not turned their encounter into an interview. He had not posed too many questions and does not know how long Anais has been divorced.

I feel the sexual excitement running through me as I anticipate meeting up with Anais later in the day. That powerful kundalini serpent, long dormant, is now coiled within me ready to strike.

I had already called my recent clients to inform them I would be stopping by with a photographer. Then, yesterday, I had my black BMW 525i detailed, and my long hair trimmed – just a bit – I never want to surrender my bohemian mien. I even purchased a new wardrobe for the day – designer jeans, black tee-shirt, gray cashmere sport jacket, and designer shoes. It's the first time I've splurged on myself in years. It feels good.

I arrive early at the rendezvous point to give myself time to think about how the day might pan out. It's a beautiful autumn day, though a bit chilly, with the Hudson valley's foliage in full bloom – making it magical and romantic. I begin to fantasize about making love to Anais, only to fall into anguish when I try to determine how to commence the seduction. I've been out of practice for years. Do I possess any charm? Am I still sexy? Being married for a score of years to an unromantic woman might have built up my desires, but certainly not my sexual acumen.

A myriad of sexual scenarios plays out in my head. Watch out for all those subtle signs, moves, words, and of course, those baiting innuendos Anais utters with her impish laugh, I tell myself. Much is said in jest – another dam cliché.

Be cool, don't move too fast. I will lose her if I miss one of her sexual overtones, and she will view me as a sensual naïf. Maintain sophistication and charm until you can peel away the thin veneer of respectability she wants to abandon, to her own chagrin.

I am a man of caution and a consummate gentleman with women. Will my good character slow the seduction to the point of turning Anais off?

My mind wanders back to my adolescence, a place I rarely tread – to misguided life lessons given by my elders. They would admonish me, believing their words had been spoken with love and concern only to advise that I should live in a fool's paradise of denial by reducing complex life decisions to silly and ridiculous sayings – and a mere flip of a coin.

"Haste makes waste," and its rebuttal, "The early bird gets the worm."

Yes, the existentialists are correct. Life is absurd, and we try to escape this absurdity with home-spun surrogate 'wisdoms' that bring smiles to our faces and chaos to our souls.

O well, I chuckle, "just go with the flow." Best I don't over analyze on a cerebral level. I will "cast my fate to the wind." Ha, ha – fucking clichés.

Elia's Journal | Friday | October 16, 1992 | 10:00 a.m.

Interlude to an Imaginary Lover
A gentle breeze disturbed her long hair
Brushing it against her innocent complacent face
Like ripples in a once tranquil pond
It cast rings about her daydream.

In her little annoyance
I saw a hidden composed beauty
That only silent and unsuspecting eyes could comprehend
A distant apart, not far,
Seemed like an eternity near
Till time ebbed
In the thunder of a single heartbeat.

Unnoticed to my eyes and thoughts
Oblivious to my presence
We passed each other in our daydreams.

A tranquil tree lined garden
Shades the emotions of a dream never to be lived
Yet lingers on like a scent of a rose
No longer in my sight.

TGIF

"Hey Elia, are you into one of your meditations or has your brain gone up into the stratosphere? Well, I do hope you are thinking of me. How do you like my new outfit from Bergdorf Goodman? I mean, does it pass as a poor bohemian, starving artist/photographer look or is it too haughty?"

I am pleasantly jolted from my reverie as I look up at Anais. She is wearing form-fitting designer jeans that define her well-formed ass, black high-heeled knee-high boots, a low-cut white lacy blouse that reveals the form of her beautiful bosoms, and a waist-high distressed leather jacket. Her thick dark hair cascades over her shoulders. She looks so hot, elegant, and inviting. Flashing her impish smile, she pulls off her aviator sunglasses.

"So, Elia, what do you think about my new outfit? After all you have an artist's eye for proportion and aesthetics."

"O Anais, it's beautiful. You have elegant taste and a bohemian heart, though your wardrobe can't compete with your natural beauty."

"O Elia, no need to flatter me, I am well beyond that phase of my life."

"Sorry Anais, I'm not a flatterer, I leave that to manipulators. I prefer compliments that are genuine and true, and intended only for the benefit of the receiver."

"Checkmate Elia. I see you have not lost your gentleman's charm and quick wit. Let's go and take some pictures of your work for your portfolio. I am waiting with bated breath to see what form of architecture your existential mind creates. Is not an architect's design an extension of his soul?"

"Why Anais, are you analyzing me?"

"Heavens no Elia, I'm just making small talk and giving you a compliment. Let me grab my camera bag from my car and I'll join you for a quick demitasse before we get on our way. It will warm me up and I need the caffeine."

When we finish our coffees, I walk Anais to my car, open the door for her, then walk around to the driver's side and enter myself. I was not expecting Anais to comment on my BMW, I know Ben is a successful businessman in the entertainment business and that Anais is conditioned to an upscale lifestyle. Her silence is my compliment.

"Anais, would you like to hear some music as we drive?"

"No, Elia, I'd prefer we talk and get to know more about each other. Why we hardly know each other, and I'm not sure where we are going, though I do trust you."

I face Anais to make eye contact. We smile at each other.

"You are right Anais we should talk. I warn you I am an honest man and a terrible liar. This accounts for my poor poker playing skills. I don't know how to bluff."

After a moment I continue, "We are heading south to take some shots of a few houses, a hospital addition I designed in Putnam County, and a historic train station I was commissioned to restore. From there we will follow the river south to Westchester, to check out a few interiors I designed. Then I will have to stop at my office to sign a few checks. After that, if you don't object, I made reservations for dinner alfresco at one of my favorite restaurants on the Hudson. Am I being too forward or presumptuous?"

"No Elia, I think it is really romantic of you."

Anais' voice takes on a serious tone. "What is your connection to the river Elia? It seems to have a powerful hold over you."

"Yes Anais, guilty as charged. I find the river to be magical, even more so mystical. It has become an extension of my soul. It talks to me in a silent language that only my soul can hear and understand."

"So, you have a deep spiritual side as well Elia?"

"You are very astute Anais, but you are only partially correct. It is not merely a side of me, it is all of me."

"O Elia, you can't for a second have me believe it has anything to do we me being astute. It's more women's intuition."

"Yes Anais, your intuition is a woman's virtue and it's astute as well."

"O Elia, checkmate."

Throughout the day as she takes photos, Anais keeps a critic's eye on Elia's work. To a degree it calls to her, like the river calls to Elia. It has an unseen power, a mystery that is whispering clues to her. She is transfixed by Elia's designs, his sense of geometry, proportion, symmetry, juxtaposition.

I love Elia's work as much as I am pleasantly disturbed by it, Anais says to herself. It is a unified contradiction, organic, eternal, as close as it is distant. I see a stark and raw nakedness, not minimalist – that's too languid, a catchall term that could never describe Elia's work. His raw and naked interiors are actually facades that hide his real self. There is something long-dormant, passionate… I am getting stimulated. Each shot I take is like a caress that envelopes me, better yet penetrates me deep in my body and in my soul. I want to know his secrets. I want to reveal his secrets, especially those he has kept from himself. Elia's work arouses my soul – one I have always denied – as well has my sexuality.

"Anais are you ready? You look like you are really into your work."

"Yes, Elia, more than you know. I am looking forward to

developing the film. I hope I've been able to capture the essence of your work. It's been no easy task Elia."

"O Anais, now who is the flatterer? It is just a combination of bricks and sticks thrown together in an attempt to create a living-art habitat in time and space. Well, enough of the lecturing, we have to make it to my office in time to sign the payroll checks."

Elia pulls his car into the driveway of a small commercial building where his office is located. It's on the second floor where many contractors have their offices. Elia introduces Anais to Liz, his office manager, as the firm's photographer commissioned to update the portfolio.

"Hello Anais, nice to meet you, can I get you a coffee?"

"No thank you Liz. I am fine."

As Liz walks away to get Elia's messages and the payroll checks for signing, Elia notices that Anais is sizing her up.

Liz returns with the payroll checks and Elia signs them immediately.

"Liz, please hand out the checks and tell the staff they are free to leave early for the weekend."

"Elia I am sure they will appreciate it. It has been a tough week for the staff with all the planning board deadlines. And if you don't mind me asking, what's with the new threads? Are you finally giving up your pin-striped suits and dressing to match your bohemian attitude? Your suits are way too rigid for your long hair not to mention your loose character. You are always a contradiction Elia.

"And before I forget, your attorney, Rit, called a few times. He said it's important to call him as soon you as you get in. A few contractors called screaming for approved shop drawings and approved pay apps. And of course, lovely Beth called about five times.

"Oh, and your reservations for next Friday night's reunion party in the city are confirmed."

"Thank you, Liz. Can I impose on you to keep Anais company for a while as I return my calls? I won't be long."

"Anais, please excuse me while I take care of some unpleasant business and re-confirm our dinner reservations for tonight."

"Sure Elia, we have time. Liz and I can bond."

After a while Elia emerges from his office a bit flushed.

"Elia are you alright?"

"I'm fine, Liz. Typical Friday afternoon contractor calls. Just lock up when you leave with the staff. Anais and I have business to discuss over dinner." He winks at Liz as they turn to leave.

"Nice meeting you Anais, enjoy your dinner. Elia we can go over the deposits and account receivables on Monday."

"Thank you, Liz. Have a nice weekend. My best to the family."

"This way Elia," the waitress says as she walks the couple to Elia's favorite table on the terrace overlooking the Hudson.

"So, Elia, they know you on a first-name basis here as well. You must be a very popular guy."

"Hardly Anais, I come here often."

"On dates?"

"I take my clients and potential clients here. It has a nice ambiance to it."

"You mean the river right Elia?"

"Yes."

"This is a very romantic place. Have you dined here often with Beth?"

"Never."

"Tell me why Elia."

"I invited her many times, but she never accepted."

"I can't imagine why not. Do you know why?"

"Beth has no aesthetic for life. Every action to her is merely a chore of life. She has a very old-world blue-collar mind set. You work in a job you hate just to pay bills. You eat just to fill your stomach. Life is just to live for utility. There are no joys, only chores. Romance is not even a chore. It is something that gets in the way of doing a chore. Even sex is a chore. She does it as a marriage chore. She makes it quick and without feeling, like eating food without salt or spices, just eat to stop the stomach from growling."

"How are you able to communicate with her?"

"We are never able to communicate. We have no dialogue, no commonality. If I attempt to talk of architecture, art, music, philosophy, theology, she views it as blah, blah ...bullshit."

"Well, what does she talk about?"

"Nothing of value, not even planning for our daughters' futures. She has a real disdain for the white-collar world, especially intellectuals. She just watches the same stupid TV shows, along with all the reruns, laughing at the punch lines as if she is hearing them for the first time. She spends hours with her friends and family talking gossip, criticizing successful people, mostly me."

"Elia, I am confused, please explain. If she is so unromantic with sexual hang ups, why is she having an affair with another man?"

"Beth never grew as a person. She stopped growing mentally at age 18. In her world people don't strive to attain higher goals and reach self-actualization. She has a fatalistic view of life, what some existentialists refer to as quietism. Basically, her mantra is, 'If other people can do it fine, but I cannot, so I try not. This is my sordid destiny, not for me or you to change.'"

"So, Elia, how did this lead to her infidelity?"

"For Beth, heading out for a romantic weekend getaway, complete with a fine upscale dinner, dancing, champagne, and a penthouse hotel room for passionate and prolonged love making Kama Sutra-style is a gauntlet she fears."

"So, Elia, what kind of man did she find as her paramour?"

"Beth found the man of her dreams, a teamster truck driver who hauls concrete to job sites. With a limited education and small radius of knowledge he does not threaten her insecurities with deep conversations or talk about the future. She needs a man who obliviously leads a stagnate life. A romantic night out for them is pasta and beer at some local pizza joint with like-minded friends, telling the same dirty jokes. They finally get shit faced enough to have a 15-minute quickie, which leaves a romantic memory that lasts until they sober up. With me, she ignored all post-sex talk or discussions about how to experiment and heighten our sensual experience."

Forgive me, I have shared far too much. It is rather inappropriate to speak ill of your ex on a first date. Anais I am not an emotional or sentimental man, rather I am a very cerebral one seeking analytical answers by always asking why?"

"No Elia, you are wrong, you didn't say too much. If you had said not one word about it, I would have figured it out just by examining your architecture. Elia, it speaks to my soul. There is a surging sexuality within you that needs to be challenged. It is as passionate as it is intellectual. It speaks to the flesh, mind, and soul. I know Elia. I know. I have experienced this sexual wasteland with Ben. He has never awakened my sexuality, even with orgasms. Sex with him is bland at best. Ben too, cannot understand the higher and refined beauty of real sexuality. For him it is simply releasing the goop the quicker the better, like stuffing food in your mouth so fast to quell your hunger that you can no longer savor its taste. It would not matter if he was eating caviar or shit. Ben grew up on the streets of the Bronx in a very dysfunctional home. Ben is street smart, savvy, and a master Svengali. He can also be brutal. He has a keen, pragmatic and malicious intellect. He is only tolerant, giving, and forgiving if it suits his goals. When he gives, it is only to receive ten-fold."

"Do you fear him? Should I fear him Anais?"

"No need to worry, I can handle him. He poses no threat to you."

"Anais, we seem to have much in common, though there is much more to know about each other".

"Agreed Elia. You have shared much of your life with me in a very short time. You are open, honest, confident, though never arrogant. Yet, with your open-book life, you still remain a mystery to me, an enigma of sorts."

"Anais, do I disappoint you? Do you think I am hiding some ominous secrets?"

"Heaven's no Elia, quite the contrary, I want you to allow me to seek them with you and within you."

"O Anais, most cryptic and seductive. Let's escape our xeric pasts to the sweet waters of the eternal river."

"O Elia, now who is being esoteric and cryptic?"

Elia pours Anais and himself another glass of the best house wine and makes a toast.

"Anais, a toast to our new quest to find each other within each other. Let the quest begin."

They raise their glasses, offering each other seductive smiles as their glasses strike.

"So, Elia, where will we commence our quest free of our past tribulations and free of any obstacles and inhibitions?"

"Join me next Friday Anais, at my reunion party in the city. The one Liz mentioned."

"Yes Elia, what could be a better starting point for our quest than a party in the city. Tell me more about it so I can plan and dress for the occasion."

"It is a ten-year reunion party of sorts with some of my fellow architects. We all cut our teeth together as architects at the same firm before we headed out on our own. The firm itself is no longer in existence though most of us have kept in touch for the sake of friendships and business contacts, mostly the latter. Some have done quite well for themselves, so we planned this big private party down in the Wall Street area at a rather expensive venue. The evening will include the standard fare, cocktails, four-course gourmet meal, live music, and of course dancing. Why don't we plan to stay out all night and book a room?"

"Yes! I guess I should thank Beth for this. After all, if she were a bit more romantic, I am sure you would not have been so flirtatious when we met last week at Karen's place."

Anais and Elia raise their glasses, "To Beth" they toast, offering each other a smile of sarcasm to reveal their contentment.

Elia takes a casual glance around the dining area and notices they are the last diners in the room. He summons the waitress for the tab and apologizes for not being more sensitive to the time.

"Anais, we should get going, the staff wants to go home. I was so caught up in our conversation I lost track of the time. Why we never even ordered dessert and our demitasse."

"I agree Elia, no problem. Can you believe we have been here for close to six hours?"

"It must mean something Anais, when two people on a shared quest can transmute time to prolong the pleasure."

"Yes Elia, it will give us time to transmute our hearts and souls alike."

Outside the restaurant in the deserted parking lot, Elia turns to Anais, "Would you like to take a quick stroll along the river path? The river is alone and seeks our company."

"Sounds quite romantic," Anais says as she takes Elia's hand.

They walk to the river and stop at the rail at the edge of the foot path. Elia gazes spellbound into the water.

"Elia, what do you see in the river? What is it saying to you?"

Elia turns to Anais, takes her in his arms and applying a little pressure to his embrace looks deeply into her eyes as he kisses her passionately. She offers no resistance, returning his kiss and embrace. Slowly they pull apart.

"Anais, the river speaks in silence."

"Elia, is that another riddle or clue for me to decipher."

"Hardly, I am as transparent as the waters of our mutual desires."

"Then Elia, we should bathe in those mystical waters. My daughters are with their father tonight. I don't believe they will be coming home. It's well past midnight and we have a ride ahead of us. Let's head to my place and continue on with our quest."

They quickly walk back to the car, consumed with passion knowing it's a long ride home.

"Elia, I travel this road often at night. I know all the speed traps and where the police hide. Don't worry if you get a ticket. Ben will take care of it."

"He would do that for me? – a man who is spending time with his ex-wife?"

"No, he'll do it for me. He is well connected if you know what I mean."

Elia red-lines his BMW and arrives at Anais' around 1:00 a.m. The house is dark. A Mercedes is parked in the driveway, so he pulls around to park in the front.

"Ben! What the 'F' is he doing here? He was supposed to take our daughters away for the weekend. He must have pissed them off, gotten into an argument or something. I'm sorry Elia. I'm not playing games. I just want for us to make real love together."

She turns to Elia and kisses him passionately. With built-up desire Elia places his hand on Anais' tight jeans and begins to massage her thigh with soft strokes. Slowly he moves his hand up her leg to her well-formed pubic mound. They are both very stimulated and oblivious of their location.

Elia places his left hand down her panties to touch and massage her yoni. Anais puts her hand on Elia's crotch, opens his zipper and feels his erection. Elia then pulls down Anais' panties with her help and begins to loosen his belt. He tugs on his trousers and underwear to pull them down. Anais grabs his naked erection as Elia continues to massage her pubic mound.

In the intensity of the moment, Anais whispers, "As you can feel, I shave. I place no veil before my intentions."

"Thank you, Anais," Elia whispers. "I never poke my head inside a closed dark curtain."

He rubs her orgasm's fluids over her mound. They chuckle. Then Elia kisses her neck, moving his hand to feel her well-formed breasts. He crunches over to kiss her thighs and moves up to kiss her yoni.

They are lost, acting out their fantasies as a light is turned on in the house.

"Elia, Elia stop! The house is up! We have to pull ourselves together. Quickly!"

They dress and regain their composure to a respectable degree before the front light goes on. Ben storms out of the house, gets into his car and races off seemingly unaware of their presence. One of Anais' daughters comes out looking a bit disturbed.

"Sorry Elia, I was hoping you could spend the night here.

Looks like Ben had one of his temper tantrums with our daughters."

The daughter acknowledges the car and starts to walk over.

"Sorry Elia, my daughters need me. I hope you understand. I look forward to next Friday. Pick a nice romantic place to stay for the night. Let's meet up at Karen's to finalize our plans."

Anais opens the car door and heads to her daughter. Looking back at Elia, she smiles, "Put on your dancing shoes."

Homeward Bound

I arrive home around 2:00 in the morning. The lights are on in the house and many cars are parked in the driveway. I enter the foyer, which is in disarray, and make my way to the living room. It is noisy and filled with a number of Beth's friends and some people I don't know, mostly couples. There are empty pizza boxes and beer bottles scattered everywhere. As I walk in everyone ignores me and I make no attempt to introduce myself. When I enter the kitchen passing the crowded formal dining room, I see Beth with her friend Sal sitting close to each other at the table. He has his arm around her. Her friends, neighbors from down the street, Tony and Maria Bevanti, are also at the table. Everyone is a bit drunk and laughing at some joke.

Sal drops his arm when he sees me. Then Tony stands up and comes over to shake my hand. Maria and Beth make nervous eye contact.

"Hey Elia, good to see ya. Looks like you've been burning a little midnight oil again. Well, since you are always working late, we thought we'd throw a little party for Beth. We invited up some friends and family to keep her company. You know my wife Maria and my cousin Sal – Beth just loves his company and all his stories as a teamster. You know Sal and I, we both belong to the same union local and work on the same construction projects. We are just one big family Elia. I mean, like we have so much in common. We are all in the construction business. Can you believe it, Italians in the construction business?"

Tony looks over at Sal. "Hey Sal, don't be such a disrespectful jamook to our host Elia. He's offered up his lovely home for us this evening. Get up and get Elia something to eat. After all, he is paying for it, ha ha ha."

"No need Tony. I picked up something to eat on my way back from the office."

"You sure? My family brought up some homemade braciole, mannigott, and pasta-vazool."

"That is so very kind, thank you, but I will pass. It's a bit late for me to be eating."

Sal stands up to make a toast as he pours everyone at the table a glass of cheap chianti. "To our most gracious and beautiful hostess Beth for offering up her home to all her paisans. Salut!"

Sal casts an evil look in my direction. He is obviously quite inebriated. "Elia how rude of you to not toast your wife."

I quickly return his serve, "Sal, how rude of you not to pour the host a glass of your cheap wine?"

Beth places her arm around Sal and pulls him back. "Elia don't insult Sal. He is our guest."

Tony grabs my arm and leads me to the living room to introduce me to his family.

"Hey Elia, let me introduce you to my other cousin, Joe."

"It's nice to meet you, Joe. I'm Beth's husband Elia. Is this your first time visiting Tony up in the country?"

"Yeah, Tony came into some kind of inheritance and the next thing ya know badda-bing, he buys a house in a new subdivision up in the country. Now he's living with all you white-collar executive snobs."

"Joe, are you not happy for Tony and Maria?"

"He thinks he's too good for us now. Hey, Beth says you're some kind of like smart guy in the construction industry. You a carpenter or concrete super? Or a project superintendent, huh?

"Thank you for the compliments Joe. No, I am an architect

with my own practice."

"So that explains your preppy wardrobe and funny accent."

Tony grabs my arm and escorts me around my own home to meet the rest of his family. I am faced with a painful parade of sarcastic and drunk interlopers before I see an opportunity to diplomatically extract myself from this crowd.

Beth approaches. Tony stands off to the side.

"Hey Elia, want to hear something funny? All of my pisans here are asking me why I married a Jew."

"Why Beth, don't your friends believe Italians can be educated and refined?"

"O fuck you Elia. They mean why can't you be more like them and Sal. They say you look down at them because of the way you speak, dress, and conduct yourself. You're too proper. You lack masculinity."

Sal walks over with his protruding gut, worn jeans, and a poor excuse for a shirt. His open collar exposes gold chains and medallions.

"Yeah Elia, your mannerisms give us a lot of agita. You're not like us. Beth needs a real man in her life. Capiche?"

"Sal, please share with me your definition of a real man. Please."

"You know, a man who works at a real job, a man's job. Who earns a union wage with double-time, who can take care of her, provide for her – a man who will care for all her needs – someone more like me."

"I see Sal. Are you saying I have not taken care of Beth and provided well for her future? My home with an in-ground pool that you are enjoying more and more each day, her expensive car and her nice wardrobe, plus my many offers to take her on romantic vacations and out to five-star restaurants – all these things are not taking care of her needs? Tell me Sal, tell me. If you are so much of an expert on women, why has your wife left you? Could it possibly be that living in the basement of your mother's house, still paying rent at age forty-five and being unemployed for months at a time, not to mention your romantic evenings of pizza and beer, make you a real provider? Beth tells me you are behind on your alimony and child support. You want me to speak your language, Sal. Was your gumad worth it? Capiche? Why do you insult our heritage by parading yourself around like a proud cafone![4] For a piece of 'O Culo[5], you reduce yourself to a l'Ommo 'e Merda.[6] Chi lascia la vecchia per la nuova sa quell che lascia ma non su quell che trova[7]. Do I still talk funny to you? Capiche pisan?"

"Hey Elia, you no capiche? I don't capiche Italian."

"Interesting Sal, you don't understand Italian and have little command of the English tongue. Now who is the medigan[8]?"

Sal pushes me hard against the wall. Beth and Tony go to restrain him, but in his temper tantrum, he grabs one of my framed sketches from the wall and slams it to the ground, smashing it into pieces.

"Bravo Sal! You flatter me, is this your first encounter with art?"

Tony slams Sal against the wall.

"Sal, say good-bye to your cordial and gracious hosts. It's time to leave. We have overstayed our welcome and disrespected their home. Maria, round up the family it's time to go. Elia, I am sorry for Sal's actions. You are a wise man. Remember what our

---

[4] "Lower class."

[5] "Ass."

[6] "Man of shit."

[7] "He who quits the old for the new knows what he has left, but not what he will find."

[8] Slang for person who is not Italian.

elders taught us when we were children, it will help you gain perspective and render forgiveness, 'Chi va con lo zuppo impara a zoppicare'[9]."

"O Elia, see what you have done! You insulted my guests and made them leave. This is why I hate you. Why can't you be more like my friends? They know how to have fun. They are everyday people, not like your arrogant self."

Beth runs to the door, "Hey Sal, call me tomorrow, we can go to the truck show at the Civic Center. I am sorry Elia disrespected you."

I look around the disheveled house. There are soiled paper plates everywhere, the furniture has been moved around and is now stained with food and wine. A lot of the artwork has been pushed over, and a number of framed art pieces are smashed on the floor. I walk to the back terrace overlooking the pool. There are empty wine and beer bottles on the pool deck. Half-empty food cartons are dispersed among discarded garments. In the pool there are chairs and deflated floats.

When I walk back to the kitchen, Beth is standing against the counter with a bottle of beer in one hand and a slice of cold pizza in the other.

"I was unaware you were planning a party for this evening. You could have at least informed me, Beth. I see you and Sal are rather close. Is there something you need to tell me or want to talk about like adults? Beth?"

"Fuck you Elia, why would I invite you? See how much fun my friends are?"

"Destructive as well, Beth! Is this your idea of having fun?"

"Yes, it is! Elia!"

"Look at all the damage they have done to our beautiful

---

[9] "He who goes with the lame learns how to limp."

home. Is this the example you want to set for our daughters?"

"They are with friends for the night. I will have it cleaned before they get home."

"Beth, are you trying to cover your tracks? This is our daughters' home too. They should not have to witness such carnage."

"No Elia, it's not their home, it's not my home, it's your fucking home. Elia, Mr. Fucking big shot architect, you had to have the large center-hall colonial with four bedrooms, in-ground pool, gazebo, and landscaped-lawn. It's all you! It's all about you, right, Elia?"

"For the record, Beth, you picked out the house. I believe you insisted on it. As you know, I wanted an artist's loft in an artist's community so our daughters could be exposed to culture."

"No! No! No! Elia, you wanted this big house so you could live in a new sub-division with your show-offy white-collar friends. Right? Elia!"

"Beth, I have lived in colonial houses all my life. This is not moving up for me. At most it's a lateral move that has taken me far from the neighborhood where I belong. I made this sacrifice for you and the family."

"Elia, do you take me for a fool with all your educated double talk? This house means nothing to me. You mean nothing to me. Capiche?"

"Do you really mean this Beth?"

"Elia, I have never been so certain in my life."

"I understand Beth. After twenty years of marriage, we finally agree on something."

I walk over to my cache and grab the divorce papers.

"Here Beth. This is your lucky day. You have been served with divorce papers."

"On what fucking grounds Elia?"

"Infidelity."

"O fuck you Elia. You ain't got no proof. Who is going to believe you? Wait until our daughters hear this one. They will think you are the crazy one not me."

"Beth, do you take me for a fool? I know what's going on between you and Sal. It's so obvious, Beth! Just agree to the divorce. The financial arrangements are generous. We will put the house that you loath so much up for sale."

"No. No! No! I have nothing going on with Sal. You can't prove it!"

"Dear Beth, you don't have any options. I hired a private investigator. We have you and Sal on film going to your favorite motel on a number of locations. Why we even have him coming to our house one afternoon when I was away on business. Would you like me to share this with our family and children? Huh Beth?"

Beth begins to cry and sob hysterically, just like the night behind the tavern twenty years ago.

"Elia, my house, my house. I love my house. My family is so proud of me. Where will I live? Where will I go?"

"Beth, since this house has brought you so much pain, you are free to move in with Sal. I am sure he will take care of you."

Beth takes divorce papers and signs them.

"I have purchased a loft and will be moving out by month's end. I will list the house with a broker."

As I retire to my study Beth and the house are left in a state of despair.

Bronson's Gift

"Reason is, and ought only to be, the slave of the passions, and can never pretend to any other office than to serve and obey them."
–David Hume

It is done. Beth has signed the divorce papers. Exhausted, I retire to my study and slouch on the leather sofa. Thoughts of Anais and the purchase of my loft are calming but the raging seas of my mind keep pondering how I fell into such an existential tailspin.

I forage deep into the vast wilderness of my reflective mind and stumble over the life event and resulting moral decision that led me to this day. My mind pauses and throws a non sequitur – "No good deed goes unpunished." I smirk, one of those damned clichés. The irony of life, no, the absurdity of life as the existentialists say.

I can recall clearly the first time I made love to Beth. It was Friday night, November 4, 1972. I was in my apartment reading "The History of Architecture," by Sir Banister Fletcher, in preparation for a college exam. I had not seen or spoken with Beth for a few months. I was not keeping count of our time apart. Since the bar event our steady relationship had been shaky. I didn't feel comfortable with her. She was never quite stable and always insecure. She needed a lot of male attention and I did not place much trust in her. I was surprised when she called me pretty much out of the blue. I was lost for what to say or how to handle the call.

"Hey Elia, it's Beth what's ya doing this evening? Just called since I didn't hear from ya in a while. What's going on?"

"Hi Beth, just hanging out at my apartment and doing some reading."

"Oh well, don't expect any company from me. I'm not coming over!"

"No problem Beth. I didn't invite you."

"Well Elia, you're so rude. After all this time you've never invited me over to your place. You got something to hide?"

"O my dear Beth, I believe you are mistaken. I have invited you over many times, even to the little apartment warming I had a few months ago. Remember?"

"No! Elia you are lying. You must have some mental problems."

"Beth, we have witnesses to my invitations. Remember?"

"No! No! No! Elia! You and your friends are all liars."

"Thanks for calling Beth. Have a pleasant evening."

I hung up the phone. After a moment the phone rang again. I assumed it was one of the guys calling to see if I was up for going out for a drink at a local club.

"Hello."

"Elia, its Beth. I'm sorry for what I said. You're right, I never took you up on your offer. So, to make it up and for calling you a liar, can you pick me up and take me over to your place? After all, I should be the first woman to see your place. Right Elia? I'll be ready in about a half hour. That should give you time to drive here. See you soon Elia."

I remember getting out of the shower and grabbing a shirt I had not worn in a while. At the time I was not sure why I had such an aversion to that expensive frilly white shirt. I should have thrown it out, but I didn't. Maybe synchronicity was at work, or maybe it was just fate.

When we arrived back at the apartment, Beth presented me with a small, wrapped gift and a very affectionate hug and kiss.

"Sorry Elia, it's your belated birthday present."

"Thank you, Beth. Let's just say it's an early gift for my next birthday, next month."

"O Elia, always the consummate diplomat. It's just a small gift, and it's the thought that counts."

I took off the wrapping and looked closely at the gift. It was a book. The subject-matter surprised me.

"Elia, of course it's a book, and on one of your favorite topics, philosophy. Do you like it, Elia?"

I reached over and gave Beth a big hug and kiss.

"O Beth. How did you know Sartre is one of my favorite contemporary philosophers?"

"Humph. I just guessed."

"A good guess at that Beth. How do you like my humble efficiency apartment? Please sit down. You have two choices, my sofa bed or the floor."

Beth walked over to the closed sofa bed. As she turned away from me, I could not help but notice that she was wearing tight form-fitting corduroy jeans and a low-cut tank top.

Beth had a beautiful and well-formed ass. In all honesty, this is what drew me to her the first time I set eyes on her in high school. She was standing near the bleachers talking with one of her girlfriends. It was her well-formed ass that grabbed my attention. In high school she was an introvert, she only had a few friends and kept her distance from people. She rarely smiled and had no interest in academics, not even a hint of interest in planning her life.

"Beth would you like a drink? I have some Southern Comfort and some white wine. Sorry, not many choices. I'm on a tight budget."

"I'll have whatever you're drinking Elia."

"Well then, a glass of Southern Comfort it is, on the rocks."

"O Elia, if you don't mind can I put on the TV? My favorite show is on tonight, Sonny and Cher. We can watch it together as we drink our Southern Comfort."

I never was, and still am not, a fan of popular culture. I have a disdain for it as much as I do clichés and adjectives.

"Yes Beth. Now how romantic is this?"

I thought I would have to endure the full Sonny and Cher Comedy Hour with their guest star Bobby Darin as they performed an operatic parody of Robin Hood.

Beth was totally immersed in the show. Half-way through she looked at me. "Elia, you are such a poor host. Can't you see my glass is empty? Pour me another Southern Comfort."

As I got up from the sofa bed, I felt something in my shirt pocket. I reached in and pulled out two pills. They were the pills Bronson had given me at our encounter in the bar parking lot. I had forgotten all about them. I had not worn this shirt since that fateful date.

"Hey Elia, whatcha got in your hand, huh?"

"Beth I'm not sure, they look like ludes."

"Elia what the hell are ludes?"

"They are methaqualone, a prescription sedative."

"Where did you get those Elia?"

"Ummmh, I can't recall. Well, it's not important."

Beth grabbed one and swallowed it. "I am feeling some anxiety. This should help me calm down and make me less hyper. So, college boy you gonna join me or what? After all they are yours. Did you ever do these before? Like what's the high like?"

"Can't say that I have. I would think they are a downer, not an upper."

"Well then, we will both be down together. Right Elia?"

My mind went into analytical and cerebral overload as my

gut twisted with some form of cosmic warning. It was a moment of decision for sure. My mind became a three-ring circus of existential thought, moral philosophy, and the desire to get laid. My mind swung like a pendulum from the extremes of the logic bandwidth. Over the past two years of our on-again off-again relationship, Beth had maintained she was a virgin and was saving herself for the man she would marry. Over those two years our sexuality was limited to me undressing her down to her bra and panties, kissing, petting, caressing and feeling her up. The farthest she had gone was letting me massage her pubic mound. Once she became over aroused, she would just stop, freeze up, and get dressed. She would then say, "It's not you."

During our off-again periods I was told she would go to parties with other guys and get shit-faced. I began to wonder if she really was a virgin. Was I a fool to believe her?

With this thought, I took the more pragmatic view. "For all the hell she put me through," I thought, "I will just screw her for my troubles. I don't want to be the courting fool who respects her phantom virginity while she is out having sex with other men and laughing about it behind my back. Let's see where it goes. This will be a moment of truth."

"Elia, Elia, are you going to take the lude so we can get sedated together?"

With my decision made and my libido in overdrive, I downed the lude. Beth got up, walked over to the Southern Comfort and poured herself another glass.

"Elia, are you up for another round?"

She poured me another glass. We clinked glasses and sat down on the sofa bed. After a few moments she lost all interest in the Sony and Cher show. She looked at me with her big, blue seductive bedroom eyes, pulled the barrette out of her long hair, shook her head hypnotically, and nuzzled up to me.

We began to kiss passionately. I had my hands all over her. I unbuttoned her blouse and threw it on the floor. Then I unhinged her bra and cupped her beautiful breasts with my hands. I began to kiss her neck, working my way down to her breasts, kissing and licking them. Beth got up and we opened the sofa bed. Falling back on it, we resumed our positions. As she lay on her back, I began to kiss and slowly feather her stomach and navel. As I worked my way down, I unbuttoned her jeans and began to gently pull them off her, exposing her long well-formed legs and red bikini panties. She kicked off her shoes so I could finish taking off her jeans.

Beth was on her back, wearing only the red panties. She looked so beautiful and sexy. I poured some of the Southern Comfort from my glass onto her stomach and into her navel. I began to lick her. Her flesh intoxicated me more than the ludes and Southern Comfort. I started to pull off her panties, slowly pulling them down her legs. I started to kiss and lick her legs working my way up to her pubic mound, which I began to massage. Then I poured Southern Comfort on her mound and began to kiss her yoni. She just lay there in some blissful hypnotic state. I turned her over onto her stomach to expose her beautiful ass.

I started to undress, throwing my clothes on the floor. I rifled through my wallet for a condom, only to realize I had left them in the car. I was far too aroused to stop and jumped back into bed. I remember condoning my decision by saying to myself, "Just cast your fate to the wind," – another fucking cliché!

Beth had her legs open as I went to massage her wet yoni. I thrust myself upon her, first penetrating her missionary style, then engaging in a litany of positions. Beth was silent, just following along. She never initiated or even attempted to hold my sex. She had a few orgasms, then after all attempts to hold back, we came together. That's when I began to ponder my fate.

Beth held me in a tight embrace. Then she began to panic. "I'm bleeding. I'm bleeding! What did you do to me? This has never happened to me before, Elia!"

"Beth, did your parents ever talk to you about the birds and the bees?"

"Ummhh, well a little. They never said anything about this. What is it, Elia? Am I sick?"

"No Beth, this happens to some women when they have sex for the first time. Go shower. There are fresh towels in the closet."

Then something strange happened. Beth became very uninhibited. She turned on the light and with super self-confidence walked across the apartment stark naked. As she showered, she began to hum. When she finished showering, with just a towel around her head, she called me over to her. I know I was not in an altered state when I approached her, but I swear she had an aura about her and a glow on her face. She smiled and hugged me.

"Hey Elia, why are you looking at me that way?"

I froze. "She is pregnant," I said to myself.

Out loud I replied, "O nothing Beth, I am just caught up in your beautiful glowing face."

To save time and to get her home quickly, I took the thruway. Beth was quiet all the way, hardly said a word except that she was cold and to turn on the heat. I dropped her off and told her I would call her the next day.

I headed back to my apartment the same way. Route 95 was quiet, so I just drove in the right lane and reflected on the evening. I berated myself for not taking the condoms out of the car when I had returned from picking up Beth. I had never done this in the past before. I really did not think anything good would come from the evening. I had assumed she would start an argument and I'd be getting her home ASAP, or that I'd have to suffer through some useless brain-dead sitcom reruns. I had never anticipated this outcome. To perk myself up, I thought, "Statistically there is only a 20-percent chance Beth is pregnant after having sex for the first time." I was not sure where I had heard it or read it. At the same time the statistic offered me a false sense of security, a voice in the back of my head said, "Abortions are illegal."

With a queasy feeling in my gut and my mind on autopilot, I drove through the dark oblivious to my surroundings. As I approached the Mamaroneck Avenue overpass before the New Rochelle toll, I saw red blinking lights on the shoulder of the road. A number of cars were pulled over to the side with the passengers milling around. I assumed the state troopers were out in force giving out tickets. As I pulled into the center lane to give them room they started shouting and waving their arms. "They must all be drunk," I thought. A crashing sound followed as my car began to shake violently and I heard my tires squeal. My car was thrown into the guardrail before it came to a crashing halt.

Yes, this was my sign; the bad omen of what was to come.

I jumped out and walked in the direction of the pulled-over cars. As I approached the crowd, one of the state troopers walked over to me and asked, "Are you okay sir? Do you need medical attention?"

I stared back, quite confused. "What happened? What hit me?"

A crowd had gathered around me. "Hey kid we were trying to warn you," one man said. "A tractor trailer ran into one of the overhead light poles sending it across all three lanes of the highway. You just ran over a metal utility pole. Wow, looks like you don't have much of a car left, bummer man."

My car was towed to a local gas station where I spent the rest of the night sleeping in my car.

One morning a few weeks later Beth called – which was quite unusual for her – to inform me she had taken the day off from work due to a stomach virus. I inquired about her symptoms. Beth said for the past few days she would vomit soon after waking, then the nausea would pass and she'd be symptom free for the rest of the day, only to repeat the same cycle the next day. She went on to say she was going to call a doctor to prescribe some medication.

I remember well that I remained calm. I knew I was experiencing a life event, and I knew what the future held. In a calm tone I told Beth, "It's not a stomach virus. You're pregnant."

She said, "It can't be, we only did it once. What will we do?"

I drove her to Planned Parenthood for a pregnancy test. She was only 19 years old, frightened, scared, and living at home with her parents.

No surprise to me, a few days later the test results came back positive. We were married six weeks later in a traditional Roman Catholic ceremony at a small chapel with some friends and family in attendance – exclusive of a white wedding dress, Beth's scarlet letter to bear.

I simper, but before I can continue on with my self-inflicted torment and reflect further on my arduous path, I am pulled from my brain virus by a loud knock on my closed study door.

Elia's Purgatorio

"Praying to his high Lord, despite the torture,
To pardon those who were his persecutors;
His look was such that it unlocked compassion."
–Dante

My eldest daughter, Christine, bursts into the room defiant of my privacy, slamming the door open in a forceful manner to share her opinions. With direct guttural language lacking all Ciceronian style, she screams at me.

"Hey Dad! Why did you make Mom cry and insult her house guests? The Bevantis had to leave because you insulted them. Who the fuck do you think you are Dad?"

"Christine, watch your tongue and respect your father. You accuse me without knowing the facts."

"No, you are wrong. Mom told me everything."

"Christine, you are entitled to your own opinions but not to deny the facts. Do you want to hear the truth Christine?"

Christine places her hands over her ears and starts stomping her feet. "No! No! No! I don't want to hear you. No! No! No! It's all lies. Sal and Mom told me everything."

"Do you believe what they say verbatim and never challenge the veracity of their statements nor take counsel with your father to find the truth of the matter?"

"See Dad, your fancy educated words and snobbery confirm it. Don't you know how much Sal and Mom despise your arrogant ways?"

"My dear Christine, how do you equate education and refinement with arrogance?"

"Because you won't be like us Dad."

"Does this make me guilty of some crime? Besides, why can't you people be more like me?"

"Dad! Do you see Sal taking his kids to museums, making them take music lessons and stupid art classes like you want us to do?"

"Well Christine, what is your preference and what are your plans for life?"

"Sal told me college is stupid, a waste of time and money."

"Christine, I understand Sal was thrown out of high school. He never graduated. Do you really believe his lifestyle is better and happier than yours? Look at what I have provided for you, your sister, and your mother?"

"O Dad, don't fuckin flatter yourself. Mom told me you never loved me, or us. You are a totally self-centered self-serving, narcissistic fuck. You do nothing for us and have no feeling for us – not like Sal does. Mom would do anything for us, unlike you. What sacrifices have you ever made for us? Mom told me you never wanted to have me...right Dad?"

"Christine, I believe it is time to tell the truth, to set the record straight. You are mature enough now to know the truth. When I got your mother pregnant, she wanted to have you aborted. She wanted to go to some back-alley hack to have an illegal abortion. I would not allow it. We argued for days. We faced difficult choices Christine, though I was committed to only one solution."

"What options? You ruined Mom's life and mine...Dad!"

"On the contrary Christine, I gave you both good lives with much sacrifice at my expense, which I don't regret."

Christine again places her hands over her ears. "No! No! No! It's another one of your white-collar elitist lies."

"No Christine, it's the truth. I have considered myself blessed every day when I see your beautiful face and smile. I know I made the right decision. It was well worth the sacrifices. This is the truth Christine. Look into your soul and ask yourself now that you are in the prime of youth and a budding beautiful woman, would you respect me more if I had had put you up for adoption? Would you want to go through life searching for your real parents, wondering why they had abandoned you? Would you rather I had not married your mother and let her raise you in her parents' house with an alcoholic grandfather and no father figure. Or should I have gone along with the abortion, never to have brought such a beautiful child into the world? Christine, I never viewed it as a decision with options. In my heart and soul, I believed, and still believe, it was the only solution. I had the power to bring a child into the world. I could not kill what I created or chose death over life and make an innocent pay for my indiscretion. Now Christine, do you still harbor such ill feeling toward your father? This is all true."

With her head down Christine walks over to me very slowly. I put out my arms to embrace her. Then she stops and looks me in the eye. "Well Dad, if you had had me aborted, then you wouldn't hear what I am about to say. Just go fuck yourself! How does that feel as your reward for bringing me into this world and loving me?"

She storms out of the room and runs down the stairs.

The Party

Anais and Elia met at Karen's Demitasse Café for coffee and to finalize their plans before leaving for the party in Manhattan.

"Elia, so sorry about the Ben thing Friday, he is quite unpredictable and can have a quick temper when he doesn't get what he wants."

"I understand Anais, our ex-spouses are made for each other."

"So, Elia, when are you going to move into your new loft? I would love to see it."

"The closing is scheduled for next Wednesday. When are you free to come by and check it out?"

"Well, how about next Friday? Will you be moved in and settled by then?"

"Hardly, the loft will need some work. I am completing the interior designs, though by Friday I should have at least Spartan living conditions."

"Humph. Well, it's a plan then Elia. We will celebrate your new home – just the two of us – next Friday. Then we can plan for your loft-warming party."

"Yes, Anais, it will be quite romantic and erotic for sure."

They smile at each other.

"So, Elia, for the drive to Manhattan, what if we take my car? I drive in the city frequently and know how to navigate it well. It will give you time to unwind. And since we don't have to be there until 6:00ish do you want to go over our checklist for the weekend?"

"Yes, reservations are confirmed for our stay at Mohonk

Mountain Resort in New Paltz. I reserved a room with a great view of the mountain lake and the 'gunks', with a check-in time around midnight and a check out time Sunday morning. This should give us time to party in New York till about 10:00ish. We can forgo any post-party gatherings. Those events can go either way. But to be honest, I find them rather snobbish, boring and show-and-tell events. I attend them only for networking. I hesitate not to find an excuse to leave early."

"Well, an evening at Mohonk Mountain will be an incentive for us to slip out early into the night. I bought a bottle of Pastis and a bottle of Absinthe - complete with wormwood to cap off the evening."

"Absinthe? I thought that was illegal in America because it's quite potent and hallucinogenic."

"O Elia, you of all people, an artist, philosopher, and romantic, have never tried it? Elia I'm surprised. Though, I will tease you a bit. It is also the drink of lovers to stir their libidos. I will share with you the secrets of Absinthe, if you will share your poems and stories of the Kama Sutra with me. I brought a few other surprises as well."

On the drive down Elia shares some insights as to what to expect at the party, and how it will be an awkward experience for him. Over the years he has attended these annual reunions without Beth. His peers always speculated as to the reason why Beth never attended. Some believed Elia was ashamed of Beth's looks. Some of the women architects surmised Beth was just a phantom person Elia had created to use as an excuse to not accept their invitations to attend the party with them - Elia's way of blowing off would-be suitors without losing his character. A few, just to be spiteful, spread rumors that he might be gay. Elia never flirted with the single women. He was always cordial and respectful, and to a degree self-effacing.

Upon hearing this Anais smiles. "Tell me Elia, why can't you disrespect people who disrespect you?"

"Anais, you can't curse the dark."

Anais chuckles. "Now Elia, are you going to hide behind the clichés you so much disdain?"

Elia smiles and laughs. "You are quite the muse. No, it's not formally a cliché, merely a spiritual mantra or axiom."

"Well Elia, I will leave it at that then. Do they know you are now divorced and have a new paramour?"

"I never mentioned it. I just marked off on the RSVP I would be attending with a guest."

"Well then, let's have some fun this evening breaking your awkwardness at the expense of your peers."

Anais is wearing an elegant black dress with a mid-thigh hemline, exposing her well-formed legs and stilettos that enhanced her 5'-6" frame. Her dress has an equally revealing neckline that complements her divine proportions. She's had her dark hair styled for the day and it graciously falls upon her shoulders like a cascading waterfall. For contradiction and juxtaposition, she wears librarian-type glasses just to tease. Elia is in one of his best blue pinstripe suits with a business power tie. His hair is well-coiffed though long and roguesque to affirm his independence from convention.

They are oblivious to the grand entrance they make, unaware that all eyes are on them. As they enter the reception area, they are greeted by Al Lombard, now a senior partner in a prestigious design practice. He was Elia's first boss and mentor. Over the years Al has put on weight, is balding, and always looks frumpy even in the best tailor-made suits.

As Al approaches them, he grabs a few appetizers from one of the wait staff.

"Well Elia, what a surprise to see you attending our annual

reunion finally with your wife. This is a first."

"Well, for the record, I am divorced. Let me introduce you to Anais."

Al is captured by Anais' beauty and slips between the couple.

"So, Anais, what a seductive name. So nice to meet you. Did Elia tell you I was his first boss and mentor and that now I am a senior partner in one of New York's most prestigious design firms? Why, Elia owes all his success to me."

"Yes, Al, Elia has shared the story with me many times."

As Anais continues the conversation Al grabs a few more appetizers from the wait staff and continues to talk, chewing his food with his mouth open.

"So, Anais, are you also an architect?"

"O Al you flatter me. I am merely a photographer and actress."

"O Anais, you are far too humble – only a photographer and actress. I would love to hear more about this. How about one day you come as my guest on my cabin cruiser, and we can chat. You could tell me more about your acting career. I am sure Elia wouldn't mind."

Al has his back towards Elia and turns to him, "Right Elia? You won't mind if Anais spends time with a real architect."

Anais takes a step closer to Elia. "Sorry Al, I am not one for the water. I easily get seasick. But feel free to check me out on cable, you never know where I may pop up. Excuse us Al, Elia and I are going to celebrate our anniversary with our first dance. Nice meeting you. I prefer to dance with a real architect and romantic."

Al leaves in a huff, pushing Elia aside as he exits the room.

"Elia, Al is quite the poacher. Is he married?"

"Al has a type 'A' personality, and no, he has never been married. It's hard to believe how such an uncouth man can make it so far up the food chain."

"Well Elia, maybe on his next boating trip Al will find a mermaid."

Elia smiles at Anais, appreciating her humor. "Better yet Anais, maybe a large tuna sushi roll. Al is more adept at handling food than women."

Anais and Elia take to the crowded dance floor for a few dances – a bit unusual for Elia's reserved demeanor. All eyes and gossipy lips are fixed on them. This is a side of Elia they have never seen before. When they exit the dance floor, two of Elia's fellow architects, and former suitors, approach them to make conversation.

"Anais let me introduce you to Stephanie and Gretchen. We started out in the same practice together after graduation."

"Hello Anais, so nice to meet you. Well, Elia, we must say this is a real surprise...finally attending our annual reunion with a female guest. This quells the rumors."

"May I inquire about what rumors Stephanie?"

"Well, you know Elia, you always attended alone. We thought your wife Beth was a figment of your imagination, or maybe she's unattractive and you are ashamed to be with her in public, or maybe you know, you're not into women. And now you show up with this beautiful woman, and the rumor mill tells us Anais is an actress."

"Thank you, Stephanie and Gretchen for your kind compliments. Let's just say I am an artist at large."

"Hey Anais, let Gretchen and me buy you a drink at the bar. We can do some female bonding. I am sure Elia would like to engage in shop talk with the guys."

"Go ahead Anais, I will make my rounds to be gracious and then I can get you at the bar and we'll head out." He whispers in her ear, "Pretty beat gathering, quite boring, time to head out soon. Let's skip dinner, we have a bit of a ride ahead of us."

Anais whispers back, "Agreed."

"So, what are you drinking Anais? Pick your poison. This is a classy restaurant with an excellent wine cellar."

"I'll have a Pastis liqueur please."

Gretchen and Stephanie look at each other behind Anais' back. Their sarcastic faces mimic what they perceive as an uppity and snobbish choice by Anais. Anais is aware these are Elia's suitors and that they have used the bonding line to dig up some dirt, with some added insult and sarcasm. She enjoys the charade at their expense.

"O Anais, Pastis? That is so like the suave and sophisticated Elia, isn't it? So, Anais, we hear you are an actress?"

"Well let's say artist at large."

"O Anais you are far too humble. Have you played in movies? Theatre? or TV?"

"Mostly cable and indie movies if you insist."

"Humph, I don't recall seeing you or your name on any of the cable shows I watch."

"Well girls, maybe you are just tuned into the wrong channels. And by the way, I will let you in on a little trade secret – it's called make-up and stage names."

As Anais continues screwing with Gretchen and Stephanie's adolescent heads, Elia finds himself backed into the caveman corner fielding a bombardment of testosterone-laced questions from his male colleagues.

"Hey Elia, nice piece of booty you got there. I take it you finally divorced Beth and found a real woman. So, Elia, how long you been fuckin her? Huh, you lucky ugly dog."

Someone else chimes in, "She's got a fine ass man, you ploughin her back yard man?" Then another, "Hey man she got some hot lips and mouth, she giving you good blow jobs? Come on Elia, loosen up Elia and stop with your gentlemanly façade. Let down your hair and be one of the guys. Must you always be the outlier?"

"Sorry guys. I don't kiss and tell. I find it insulting to Anais. Thank you though for your compliments of sorts."

"O Elia, you just don't know how to bond with the guys."

"I am sorry I disappoint you, but for the record I bond with gentlemen, not cavemen."

"O Elia, is that the liquor talking? Why look guys, Elia even has a glass of wine in his hand. This is another first for Elia. Hey Elia, looks like you've been going down on her mound and caught a terminal case of pussy fever. Ha, ha, ha. Well Elia, look at the bright side, this dispels all the rumors we spread that you may be gay."

"Hey Elia, don't worry about the pussy fever, we hear it's common with you I-talians. Better known as the guinea flu. Capiche Elia? Ha, ha, ha, ha. What do you have to say now Eeelllleeeya?"

"Hey Sullivan, is it true what they say about the Irish male curse? Huh, is it true Sully?"

"What Irish curse? I don't know what you are talking about Elia?"

"O, you must know. You know that an Irishman's dick is smaller than his brain! Ha, ha, ha Sully. Capiche? I am talking your language now. When's the last time your wife gave you head? Does she only permit missionary style? Huh?"

"Hey Elia, watch your tongue, you're talkin about my wife."

"Why Sully, you can't take a dose of your own medicine? You know what's good for the goose is good for the gander. You know Sully, the golden rule, just let your hair down and be like one of the guys. Have I made my point Sully? Now what was it you were saying about Anais?"

The cavemen just walk away. "Those dam clichés," Elia thinks. "I do have such a disdain for them, but they are powerful weapons when used against the profane."

Anais approaches Elia, "Hey Elia, I think we overstayed our welcome. We both know what time it is. Looks like you fared no better than I. You know Elia, in a way you should be grateful for Beth, for using her as the excuse to not attend these functions with Stephanie and Gretchen – high maintenance and insecurity. They would be a poor fallback romance for you. Believe me Elia, as a woman I know. They are better suited for each other, or better yet for Al Lombard."

"Right Anais. It's pushing 10:00, let's head to our weekend getaway."

The Mountain Top

"Time is the mountain of life we climb
Upon whose precipice we humbly cling."

Anais and Elia settle into their duplex mountain-view suite with wood-burning fireplace, wet bar, king-size bed, and Jacuzzi.

"Hey Elia, I brought you a little something to make our romantic getaway even more special. I hope you like it."

Anais hands Elia a gift-wrapped bottle with a card. Elia opens the card, reads it to himself, then casts his Cheshire smile on Anais, "Ahh, nice touch Anais, you nasty little girl. Your desire will be my pleasure."

"Elia, you always know what to say. Now, unwrap your gift."

Elia pulls the wrapping off the bottle. It's the Absinthe Anais had mentioned earlier. He studies the label.

"This is illegal in the United States and not available here."

"Now you have the chance to savor it, Elia."

"Honestly, I always wanted to experiment with it. This is potent stuff. Where did you get it?"

"Let's just say Ben is a bit connected if you know what I mean. He had a case or two smuggled in from France by his Sicilian connection. It was a payback."

"Anais, need I worry for my life? Is Ben the jealous type?"

"Elia, Ben is not jealous of my relationships. He has been fucking wannabe actresses since the day we were married. So, enough of this talk. You must know Absinthe is the preferred drink of artists, especially the existential philosophers. And, of course, it's a great aphrodisiac. I will prepare the Absinthe. Can you throw a few logs on the fire and light a few candles?"

"Elia, we have both waited long for this day, and our sacrifices and longings have come to an end. Let us free ourselves this evening and deny no truth or desire. Let's speak without inhibition. I want real love-making just as you do."

"Was Ben ever, at any point during your years together, a good lover?"

"Ben does not know how to make love to a woman. He claims he loves women because he has screwed so many, but in reality, he fears them. He is afraid to get close to any lover because he knows it won't take them long to expose his vulnerabilities and insecurities. For Ben love and sex are merely a goop mill – the quicker the orgasm the better, and the more the merrier no matter how short lived. He is selfish and only concerned about himself. He is rough and crude – one orifice is just as good as any other. And he is terribly inhibited. Ben's Armani façade conceals his shallow footings. It is only my unfulfilled fantasies that have kept me sane."

Anais walks over to Elia with the two glasses of Absinthe.

"I am sorry Elia. I have said too much, and I am killing the mood. Let's make a toast."

"On the contrary Anais, you have removed the shackles of my reservations and freed my imagination. Now a toast to our new sexuality!"

They clink their glasses and sip the Absinthe.

"Well Elia, what gifts will you surprise me with? Excuse me while I go change into something to tease your existential libido."

Anise enters the bath to ready herself while Elia pulls himself together. They are both aroused with sexual anticipation.

Anais approaches the bed. She is wearing a sheer gossamer robe down to her ankles that easily reveals her lacey underwear and bra. She is wearing stiletto heels, a choker, and gold hoop earrings. Her dark hair falls upon her shoulders as she walks across the room with poise and grace. She stands before Elia with her glass of Absinthe in her hand.

"Let's drink up, it's an aphrodisiac."

Elia lights the sandalwood incense burner and opens a small bottle of lavender to sprinkle on the pulled-back sheets.

"Elia what are you doing?"

"Anais, lavender and sandalwood are the aromatic scents for lovemaking. They are aphrodisiacs of the soul."

Sitting next to each other on the edge of the bed, Elia and Anais begin to soft kiss to excite and prolong their lovemaking. Elia slowly pulls Anais' robe from her shoulders and down her body, making sure the fine silk teases her soft skin with each move. They fall back on the bed and continue soft kissing as they finger stroke and explore each other's bodies. Elia feels the goose bumps on Anais' skin as he kisses her neck, moving down to her firm and well-formed breasts. He removes her bra, kisses her breasts and licks her aroused nipples. He then places some Ylang Ylang-scented oil on her nipples and moves downward to kiss her stomach. When Elia reaches her navel, he pours a few drops of Absinthe and starts to lick it. Anais begins to giggle. Elia stops to admire her well-formed body.

"Elia, what are you doing?"

"Just a little omphaloskepsis."

Anais giggles with delight as Elia begins to kiss her thighs.

"Elia, do you think you are the only person in the world who owns a dictionary? Why do you like gazing into my navel?"

"Why Anais, it's mystical."

They both giggle as Elia removes Anais' laced thong. Elia strips himself of his undergarments and lies face to face with Anais. She has a childish smile on her face.

"Elia, tell me, why is my navel so mystical?"

"In Yoga it is considered the area of the powerful Manipura Chakra."

Anais softly places her hand on Elia's sex and looks him in the eye with a smile. "Elia, you shave!"

"Anais, I place no barbed wire before my lover."

They laugh like little children, embrace and kiss.

Elia massages some Ylang Ylang on Anais' perineum as he probes her body. Anais is beginning to feel highly aroused, though quite comfortable and relaxed. Elia massages her pubic mound with Absinthe, then gently slips his right index finger into her anterior vaginal wall in search of her most sensitive spots. As he slowly probes and massages her, she spreads her legs and releases nectar during her arousal.

Anais inquires in a whisper, "Elia, tell me about the Kama Sutra, what's it all about?"

"Anais, it's simply having the strength to surrender to each other. It is not for the profane or weak hearted. To achieve the highest levels of sexual ecstasy and consciousness, we must both surrender to each other without inhibition. Sexuality should never be reduced to a politically correct gender war. We must leave that to fools and the insecure egoists who define their sexuality via pop culture and the worthless magazines they read."

These are the words Anais wants and needs to hear, especially in light of Ben's bestial sexuality. In the past she felt challenged about receiving oral sex. She was too self-conscious of her body and her scent, having been traumatized by Ben.

Elia begins to kiss her neck and slowly moves down her body, kissing her navel as his left hand massages her nipples and his right hand grabs her well-formed ass. As he moves down to her lower stomach, Anais spreads her legs, and raises herself up at the waist. She places her hands around Elia's long hair and whispers in his ear.

"Elia, I surrender. Restrain me. I fear not your pleasures."

She hands Elia a cord.

"Elia, I trust you."

Elia takes the cord and restrains Anais' hands to the brass bedposts as he straddles her.

Elia moves down her body with slow kisses and soft body strokes as he descends upon her pubic mound. Anais now freed of her inhibitions by her restraints, opens her legs for Elia to savor her overflowing love-temple. They engage in the act of cunnilingus. Elia engages Anais' flexuous body by taking hold of her feet to bring her knees to her shoulders to penetrate her for the first time. Anais places her ankles around Elia's neck and presses her thighs in an erotic grip. Elia responds with deep circular penetrations. As she spreads her legs wide, he falls upon her missionary style for their mutual orgasm.

Elia lies at Anais' side kissing her softly across her body to tease her. She sighs in contentment. Elia removes the restraints and Anais responds by turning Elia on his back. She begins to massage some Absinthe over his body in slow deliberate sensual strokes. She kisses his neck, slowly descending to his sex. She massages his lingam with the Absinthe, then takes it to her mouth in an act of fellatio.

They caress in silent rapture as they watch the break of dawn illuminate their mountain view.

Anais prepares a scented bath for the both of them. Now feeling very comfortable with each other, they also seem to be able to read each other's sensual wants. They wash each other as they whisper their love songs, kissing, caressing, and toweling each other off. They go back to the bedroom and give each other a massage. They are preparing themselves for another evening of continued romance by building up their anticipation and desire. They dress and go into town to check out the bookstores and antique shops. After stopping for lunch at a health food restaurant, they walk the rail trail hand in hand.

Elia is a believer that true lovemaking is not limited to intercourse and does not start in the bedroom. Rather true lovemaking starts with the foreplay of spending time together walking, meditating, talking, and reading. Anais and Elia spend the day as teenagers falling in love for the first time. They are oblivious of time, space, even reality. They head back to their room to ready themselves for a 7:30 dinner reservation at the hotel.

At dinner Anais and Elia initially do not talk about the previous evening's romantic interlude. Their mutual quietness and smiles speak of their satisfaction and help to build their anticipation for the coming evening's sexual play.

"So, Elia, will your loft be ready for us next weekend? I can't wait to see it."

"The contractor is scheduled to be completed next week with the installation of the skylights and the finishing touches on my library. The move-in is scheduled for Wednesday and my new pieces of furniture are expected to arrive on Friday morning. Will Ben be alright with watching your daughters for two weekends in a row?"

"Won't be an issue, the girls had another argument with Ben, so they are spending the weekend at a friend's house. So, what time should I come by?"

"Friday afternoon, say 5:00ish."

"I can't wait. I am looking forward to seeing how you artists/intellectuals live. I will bring a house-warming gift or two."

Anais gazes at Elia with a seductive smile.

"So, Anais, I did not know you are into bondage."

"Hah, Elia. My, my how easily you took the bait. I would say you are a bit more experienced at this than you will admit."

"First time Anais, scout's honor. I'm a fast study. Was this your first time experimenting?"

Anais smiles back. "Girl scout's honor, first time. Elia, I want to live my sexual fantasies not just keep dreaming them as reruns. I feel very comfortable, safe, and open with you." She wonders to herself how a gentleman can be such a seductive lover.

"Then Anais, we will live them together."

"So, Elia, what fantasy can I give you?"

"I believe last evening was my fantasy."

"O Elia, I don't believe that for one moment. You are far too creative and sensual for me to believe that. Must I pull your fantasies out of you, for you to see? Huhh?"

Speaking in a low, seductive tone Anais says, "So professor Baldesarre, what can I do to get a better grade? I worked so hard on my studies and failed. O professor I'll do whatever you tell me to do. Teach me professor, teach me the Kama Sutra. Will you help me in my time of need? Will you punish me if I fail? Professor? So, what do you say professor? Humm?"

Elia, playing the part of the perfect muse calls out, "Waiter, check please. We'll skip desert. I have a lecture to present."

Anais and Elia look at each other and smiling and laughing with delight head to their room arm in arm.

They spend the night making love, experimenting with new sensual curiosities and role playing. Anais plays the submissive to dominate both their fantasies. They have the virility and lustiness of teenagers, coupled with a mature sexuality that leads to multiple orgasms and higher levels of consciousness. They can hear and feel the angels' wings fluttering to cool their boundless passions and desires.

As they lay naked in bed in a caress of fatigue, Anais breaks the silence.

"Elia, it gets better all the time. What can we possibly do to top this for next week? Elia, I am sure you will come up with another bold fantasy, for sure."

Anais smiles and places her hand on his chest.

"Anais, your lovemaking has such a soft touch, more so than other women. I feel a very different feminine energy in your body, most desirable, complete, and so willing to satisfy."

"Well Elia, can we talk? You know we agreed to be honest and transparent, and we have only known each other for a few weeks. I was not expecting to grow so close to you so fast. You have some kind of spiritual pull over me that I can't explain."

"Anais, is that a complaint or a compliment?"

"Elia, a compliment of course, but I have a conundrum to share with you. Before I do, can I ask you a sensual question?"

"Sure, what's on your mind?"

"Well Elia, I have been sharing my sexual fantasies with you, which you gladly entertain to our mutual satisfaction. But you have never shared your fantasies with me. I know you are not inhibited, but are you too much of a gentleman that you feel you may offend or compromise me with your fantasies? Let me guess what I believe your fantasy is, and I will grant it as you have entertained mine. Fair enough Elia?"

"Fair enough Anais."

"Well, have you ever experienced a ménage-a-trois?"

"I can't say that I have."

"Well Elia, would you like to have one? My treat."

"Anais, what heterosexual male would turn down this offer? But explain to me what this is all about."

"Well, remember that audition I went to the first day we met?

It was a nude scene. I thought it would be my last chance to be in a movie with some visibility and recognition. You alright with this so far?"

"No problem at my end."

"Well, that's not all, there is a love scene as well. You okay with this?"

"No problem. Who is the lucky man?

Anais pauses for a moment. "It's not a man, it's with another woman. Are you okay with this Elia? The audition was planned months before we met, and we met by chance."

"I understand Anais. How did you feel about doing the scene?"

"You know I always say Ben has a crude and rough sexuality. It is at best like dealing with a hairy beast with mauling paws. So, I was in search of a more sensual and emotional sexuality. After the audition, I had sex with Morgan the director. What do you think Elia?"

"Ahhh, Il mondo e bello perche vario."

"Elia. English please. This is no time to be evasive. What does it mean?"

"Simply that the world is beautiful because it is varied."

"Well, after we made love, we agreed to do it again in the near future. So here we are you, me, and Morgan all wanting to make love. So, to be fair, I will make this your fantasy come true, and we can both be engaged in an infidelity at the same time. We can enjoy it without any taboos or hang ups. Hey Elia, I owe you one. You up for it?"

"Anais, can you tell me a little more about Morgan? I know nothing about her, what she's all about. We have never meet each other. How will this impact your relationship with her? This is a fantasy for sure, but I need to know more about her. What is she into? And besides, I don't even know what she looks like."

Anais pulls out a few photos of Morgan – a bit revealing to say the least.

"Elia, here are a few pictures I took of Morgan the day of my audition. There is no debating her beauty, correct?"

"Agreed Anais, she is a beautiful woman. Tell me more about her."

"Morgan is dedicated to her profession as a director and takes on the artist's persona without reservation. Whatever she commits to she does to the fullest, playing the part without compromise. For Morgan, the bisexual experience is all part of her embracing the aesthetic of being in show biz. If she had a religious epiphany and decided to become a nun, she would embrace the faith without compromise as well – even give Mother Theresa a run for her money. That is what she is all about. In her lovemaking she is soft and tender. She enjoys the sensations and art of the act. She never views it as a competition, nor uses the bedroom as a battleground. She has a heightened and mature sexuality. If you enjoy making love to me, you will certainly enjoy Morgan's lovemaking. So, what's next Elia?"

"Do you or Morgan see a moral issue with this ménage-a-trois on any level? Are you totality comfortable with it?"

"None whatsoever, Elia, you are over thinking the offer. Are you in?"

"No problem on my end. What's Morgan's take?"

"She's in. We agreed to it on Thursday. She is very interested in meeting you."

"You do your homework well Anais."

"Well, I have a demanding professor I must satisfy."

"So, when will this take place?"

"Elia, Morgan will join us next Saturday at your loft."

The Loft

This is my first time at the loft. When I arrive, the door is open, and I see the construction crews busy at work. I see Elia and what appears to be the construction superintendent and a construction worker standing over a workbench discussing the plans.

Elia is a fanatic about details. He gets fixated on design elements that most people would not pick up on or even notice. For Elia, every detail is a piece of the mosaic, if one is missing, he says it is like a beautiful smile missing a tooth. Elia sees me at the door. He smiles at me warmly and waves me over.

"Anais let me introduce you to Miguel the millwork contractor and Luis the painting contractor. We are just going over some last-minute details and the punch list – the demons are in the details. The work should be completed by the end of the day."

Elia with his keen eye notices I am dressed to the nines and have caught the eye of every construction worker at the loft. We are amused watching their voyeuristic eyes as they ogle me.

"Elia looks like you are busy. I will head out to do some shopping and pick up a few things for this evening's ...ummhhh housewarming. I'll be back around 7:00ish."

As I am about to leave, Sal walks in with Elia's two daughters, neither of whom I have met.

"Anais, before you leave, let me introduce you to Sal and my two daughters, Christine and Sarah. Sal, Christine, Sarah, I would like to introduce you to my friend Anais."

"So, what kinda name is Anais?" Sal asks. "Sounds like anise, you know, the stuff we eat after we eat too much and get agita. Yeah, it's also called fennel. So, your name means fennel? It's a funny name, almost as funny as Elia."

"Well actually, Sal, it's Persian in origin and means water goddess. It became popular after Anais Nin wrote her erotic classic 'Delta of Venus.'"

"Erotic, huh, like does she write for Penthouse?"

"No Sal, I am referring to erotica not pornographic smut."

"Ahhh, tits and ass are all the same regardless of how you write about them."

The girls laugh, believing Sal is very humorous.

"So, Sal, is your formal name Salvatore?"

"Uhh, yea, when I was a baby everyone called be Sallie because of my curly locks. Only Elia, calls me Sal."

"I see Sallie, though I have to admit it sounds a bit feminine for a teamster truck driver, especially now that your locks have turned into a receding hair line."

"That's because of mya high testosterone levels. It's a sign of my manliness. I'm not lika Elia who wears his hair long like a woman because he's no man."

"How can you say that Sallie? I find him to be quite a man."

"Ahh fangool! What woman would want him?"

"Only a beautiful goddess of grace Sallie."

Elia inserts himself into the conversation, "Excuse me. Would you like a tour of my artist's loft?"

"Huuh, artist's loft. Looks like a factory or a warehouse. Only a gavone would be stupid enough to buy this and call it a home," Sal says. "Justa looka, no wood Formica countertops or oak kitchen cabinets, no wood paneling, just brick walls and concrete floors."

"Sal, I am sorry to disappoint you, I am sure it pales compared to your basement apartment with those panoramic views of the window wells."

Sal just cowers down, not knowing how to respond.

Elia catches the smirk on my face. "So, girls what brings you here today?"

"Christine responds, "Mom sent us over to pick up the check. You got it?"

"Yes, I do. I was planning to drop it off later today, along with the guitar I bought you for your birthday and Sarah's paid in full one-year scholarship for the gallery art school she expressed an interest in."

"Well just give us the check! You can keep the stupid guitar!"

Sarah interjects, "Yea Dad, and keep that stupid scholarship as well. Mom and Sallie said you are just trying to manipulate us and buy our love. And besides, of what value are they, Dad!? Why Sallie has taught us how to do oil changes, fix flat tires, and how to tape and spackle."

"Yes girls, important life skills they are."

Elia removes the check from his jacket pocket and hands it to Christine. Christine grabs it.

Then Sal chimes in again, "Hey girls let's pick up your Mom, cash the check, and go out for calzones, pizza, and beer."

They turn their backs on me and Elia and walk out.

I look at Elia, who is doing a poor job of acting indifferent. I give him a little hug and kiss. "Elia, see ya at 7:00. I'll be back with the Absinthe and a surprise or two."

I am taken aback by Elia's daughters' behavior. How can they disrespect him and idolize that clown Sallie? I cannot believe they are his children, especially with their lack of appreciation for art and culture. Are they really his? How stoically Elia handled the insults. Well, "you can't curse the dark," ugh, another of those dam clichés Elia loathes, though I have to chuckle at myself to make sense of the whole matter.

As the construction crews pack up and get ready to leave, a cleaning lady comes to add the finishing touches. I retire to my library and stand by the window to gaze into the Hudson River. My reverie is broken by a knock on the door. It's the moving company dropping off my furniture. With some time on my hands before Anais' return, I set the new furniture in place and hang some of my artwork. I then shower and dress for my evening with Anais.

To pass the time before her arrival I go to my library and pick out Soren Kierkegaard's *The Seducer's Diary*.

In anticipation of this evening's lovemaking, I find myself bored with my read. With my libido and kundalini energy redlining each uncontrollable fantasy, I make my daily journal entry.

Elia's Journal | Friday | October 23, 1992 | 6:30 p.m.

Sin
Lambent thoughts of desire
In whose garden kindles the flames
Of a raging fire.

Whispering temptations that prey upon our souls
Now weakened by virgin desires to touch and to behold.

Smiles of sweet deceit place sensual lips
Upon once innocent thoughts
With its carnal seeking breath
Is where sins our wrought.

A sword of contradiction
In whose lush hands of pleasure we bear
Blade of truth
With fledging desires
Is the confession we bear.

A solitary secret that speaks a legion of tongues
It's that unbound demon
Whose time has come.

Like subtle drops of passionate rain
In whose deluge
We seek not the strength to refrain.

The kiss of our hidden intimate desires
From lips that ignites a confession's fire.

Elia greets me at the door. I am wearing one of my favorite boho outfits, a loose-fitting patterned dress with frills of sorts ending a few inches above my knees. I have accessorized it with distressed knee-high boots and a scarf wrapped wantonly about my neck. My hair is manicured to look disheveled and falls just short of my shoulders. A bandana rounds out my textile persona. Even my jewelry is hand-crafted bohemian. I carry a rather large, leather bag slung over my right shoulder with the strap crossing my breast. I have on a pair of non-descript glasses that I hope make me look intellectually sexy.

"Right on time as usual Anais."

"I never tarry when romance is involved. My foreplay begins with my first knock on the door."

"For sure Anais, to delay the orgasm is to expedite lovemaking."

As we enter the loft, I drop my bag on the dining room table.

"Elia, I brought a few gifts for us to enjoy."

I pull out a half-empty bottle of Absinthe and two small, gift-wrapped packages.

"Anais, are these for me? Should I open them now?"

"No Elia, they are for the both of us. We will open them later. The curiosity will heighten our foreplay and lovemaking."

"Yes Anais, true lovemaking is predicated on curiosity and the need to explore."

"So, Elia, give me the full tour of your new artist's loft. Looks rather grand I would say. I don't recall ever seeing a triplex loft complete with three-floor clear story windows. It has an entrance on two floors and a bath on each floor. Elia, do you really need all this room?"

"Easily, and then some. Anais, can I impose on you to fix a few Absinthes while I make a call to my client and friend Steven Carroll? He is the CEO of Saint Dymphna's. I will meet you in the art gallery."

"Elia, for heaven's sake. I didn't' know your loft has a private gallery. Can you tell me what floor it's on?"

"O sorry, I forgot. It's on the third, next to the library."

"Library!"

I walk into the high-ceilinged gallery that takes up two floors, sipping my illegal Absinthe. Elia is in his study talking to the client.

Again, I can't help analyzing Elia's designs. His signature is a cold naked interior free of any finishes to hide structural functionality. He even exposes the mechanical systems, never muting them, often drawing attention to them, revealing them as he does the bowels of his soul. Elia and his work are a transparent singularity ensuring no one will ever wrongly guess his intentions. For Elia, hiding one's intentions is an admission of guilt and a suppression of truth. The small architectural details that he labors over are just like scribble marks one draws when they are bored. Elia is saying with his details, "See my scribbles. They are here. I am as bored as the designer as you are as the observer." Even his sketches are small light scribbles on a broad white pad that say, "I am here, that is all that matters. I am merely marking my existence; my essence will be found in hindsight."

Elia has this laid back, cool, and calm demeanor about him. He is never arrogant. Though each one of his words, movements, and actions are calculated gestures intended never to compromise his character, nor insult those who surround him. If he is ever attacked, his quick-witted responses are flung like the little stones from David's sling that toppled the mighty Goliath. I think this demeanor will bode well with Morgan, who enjoys the company of disciplined epicureans.

While Elia is preoccupied with his business call, I take it upon myself to tour his cavernous loft. I venture across the hall to check out the library. Aside from the bathrooms, and to a degree the kitchen, the library is enclosed in a decorative concrete block wall with intermittent details – Elia's scribbles, which I am able to understand and articulate. There is a balance and beauty to the stark rawness, like a beautiful nude woman at rest wearing only a scant of gold jewelry in select erotic locations on her well-defined geometry. There are expansive French doors flanked by Egyptian columns that I imagine are reminiscent of ancient Alexandria which held the lost library of antiquity. The French doors are lit and inviting, though the doors are locked. Above the doors the words "this is a non-lending library" are etched into the entablature. Elia guards his books jealousy, to the point of being possessive. I peer through the doors into the lit library and see a rather large skylight located in the center on the ceiling. It is directly positioned over a granite conference table with many books strewn across it, arranged in an unconscious pattern and confirming that Elia's mind never rests, even when he is not consciously thinking.

I wander into his bedroom. It is open with a view of the two floors below. This too has a skylight arranged directly over the king-size platform bed. The blankets and sheets are drawn in perfect symmetry. I feel the satin sheets and smell the scent of lavender. Elia never misses a detail.

When I hear Elia's footsteps approaching, I walk on the double-click back to the gallery, making sure I arrive ahead of him and he sees me viewing his artwork.

"My apologies Anais, I had to take this call. The CEO just informed me that my design for the Saint Dymphna's Hospital Behavioral Health Care Wing is up for a rather prestigious architectural award. Well, Anais, I have you to thank. It was your photos of the completed project that the board used to submit an application to the jury."

"O Elia, I can't take any credit for this. It is all your doing. I am just a curious and innocent bystander."

"Anais never compromise your talents. The world will easily do that for you."

"Elia, you know when I took those photos of the hospital something powerful came over me. I just can't explain it. I also noticed how all the patient rooms are laid out with beautiful views of the Hudson River. When we were there, I saw you gazing out the window as if you were looking for someone to appear. You were in a trance-like state, as if the river was talking to you. A few times I had to break you from your reverie. At first, I thought you were just one of those geniuses always off in some lofty place in your boundless brain. But there is something more to this Elia. Tell me. I know you are a man of no hidden agendas or ill intentions, but I have to know for the sake of our relationship. What is this thing you have with the river and with Saint Dymphna's Hospital? When I was at your office and just looking around, I heard Liz say to one of the architects that you had waived your commission on the project and that you were burning the midnight oil to keep payroll costs down. What's the story Elia? Please Elia, I don't see you as a self-righteous and wannabe martyr looking to get stoned for cheap sympathy. I see you as an honorable man Elia. I shared my pain and fantasies with you without regret or reserve. I ask that you be as candid with me. It's important to me Elia. I have to know you better to break you from the enigma that surrounds you like a shadow."

Elia, you have given me all I want and more, turning my pain into emotional pleasures. You are a generous giver and listener, never judgmental. Now please let me give back to you and help to heal your pain. We can heal each other Elia."

Elia slouches over and takes my hand as we sit together on a cozy couch in the gallery overlooking the river. He raises his glass of Absinthe and makes a toast.

"Anais, the truth will set us free. You are right, we must be totally honest and transparent with each other."

Elia turns to look directly at me.

"Well Anais, if you must know, yes the river is very sacred to me, and Saint Dymphna's Psychiatric Hospital holds a special place in my heart, a bitter-sweet place at best. It's a place I fear to visit, and equally a place that brings me greater pain if I don't visit every day. You see, when I was young, I had an uncle I was very close to. He was a Jesuit priest, a learned man, professor, and intellectual; his greatest virtue was that he was a humanitarian. He was consumed with making the world a better place to live. He was committed to straightening out the crooked timber of humanity, a humanity in distress. The wars, killing, poverty, bigotry, social injustice, and so on – the list of humanity's sins is endless."

He would let me sit in on his college lectures when I was in middle school. I would skip class just to attend his lectures, sometimes having to hitchhike my way there and back. After his lectures we would go out for coffee and have some great intellectual discussions. He did all he could to shelter me from my toxic parents and their abuse. He then fell into a deep state of depression, the material world had overcome him. He felt helpless, the more he tried to help humanity, the more it became hell-bent on destroying itself. One day some people found him standing by the river talking to it and waiting for an answer. They called the police, who knew him well, and they took him over to Saint Dymphna's where he was admitted for observation. During the night, he snuck out, walked over to the river and jumped in. They found his body floating in the water by Cold Spring. He had left a suicide note addressed to me. I carry it with me always and I read it every day. Do I do this to inspire myself to do good or just to torture myself? I'm never sure. I feel I owe it to him out of respect."

I received the call from the morgue to come and identify the body. When I arrived, the coroner gave me the suicide note, with instructions from my uncle to never share it with anyone – a promise I have never broken. On his remains was his red ruby graduation ring. He always told me he wanted me to have it, and to wear it as a memory of our friendship. I was overcome with grief. The coroner left the room so I could pull myself together in privacy. When he returned, he handed me my uncle's ring. I took the ring and placed it on my finger. I have not taken it off since."

In his will my uncle left me money for my college education up to the PhD level, and then some to prepare me for life's arduous path. So, Anais, this is my story."

I began to cry, and for the first time we shared our emotions. I was quite surprised to see this side of Elia as he shed a few tears from his otherwise emotionless existential façade.

"Elia, that is a beautiful story. It explains much and identifies you. Is this the reason you had to have this loft in this location?"

"Yes Anais, I believe it will bring closure to my life."

I take a deep breath and sigh, snuggling close to Elia.

"Elia, when we make love you talk about what it means to orgasm together. You said it's when the soul and the flesh in both of us come together – a spiritual orgasm. Elia, you know I am an atheist, an agnostic at best, but I must confess when you shared this story with me, I felt my soul move. It was not my heart that moved, it was my soul. I am learning now how the heart responds only to the pleasures of the flesh."

"Yes Anais, the flesh is temporal and corrupt, it is only a mortal median to use as a catalyst for us to find our divine eternal souls."

I hesitate but cannot resist returning to events from earlier in the day.

"Elia, it's not my place to interfere with your family life, but I have to say I was quite taken aback by how your daughters disrespected you today, especially in front of Sal. I don't get it. How can they say such awful things about you? You have done so much for them. I just can't understand their disdain for education, the arts, and culture. How can they look up to someone like Sal? Elia, your daughters are so unlike you. What happened to them? Did they totally miss out on your gene pool? I am beginning to believe they are not your children.

"So, Elia, why don't you try to intercede, try to talk some sense into them? They are both beautiful young women. Why, with your successful practice and business contacts, aren't they smart enough to know that you can position them well in life? What gives Elia? Why are you just sitting back and letting Sal set them up for failure?"

"Chi si accountenta gode – those who are content with what they have, enjoy what they have."

I smirk, "So Elia are Italian cliché's exempt from your existential philosophy?"

"Chi si scusa s'accusa."

"Elia, please, in English."

"He who excuses himself accuses himself. Anais, I offer them a banquet of caviar and champagne, they clamor for beer and calzones. They can't comprehend or appreciate the aesthetics of life. They see my advice as preaching and being manipulative, and Sal's words as gospel. Beth and Sal have a small radius of thinking. Beth has a high school diploma. Sal is a drop out. She is not threatened by him and feels comfortable with him. Beth knows if I can influence Christine and Sarah to make something of their lives, she will feel like she is losing them. So, she smothers them with ignorance to keep them in the dark and in her possession. She is committing emotional and intellectual homicide. It's cowardly. She is letting Christine and Sarah take the bullets for her."

"Elia, there has to be something you can do before that Sal ruins your daughters' lives."

"There is nothing I can do until they witness the day when Sal ruins Beth's life, takes her money, and leaves her. It's all part of their illness."

"What illness Elia?"

"For one, insecurity, and it's contagious. They are living in Plato's cave. It's their sanctuary."

"Elia, what about their future?"

"Anais, they are living their future in the present. Merely existing is their essence."

"Well Elia, then we will plan for our own future. I really want to do something nice for you. Do you have a current passport?"

"Why yes. Why do you ask?"

"Well, when I was around and about this afternoon, I booked us an extended romantic weekend at a private resort in Martinique, all expenses paid thanks to Ben. I booked it on Ben's credit card. He will thank us for the tax deduction.

"Elia let's forgo our dinner plans at the Thai restaurant across the street tonight and take the express to your bedroom. I hunger for your soul. I want to heal you as you heal me. But first, will you join me professor for some aqua erotica in your oversized footed bathtub? I prepared a special bubble bath for us with scented water and seductive oils."

I strip in front of Elia to tease him. I am the tempting siren now in control of Elia's passions.

Elia stands fixated as his eyes pan my smooth legs, well-formed ass, and breasts with erect nipples.

"Professor, let's transmute our fantasies into our reality today to ensure we both create the most fond and erotic memories for our future."

I walk over to Elia, nuzzle up to him and whisper in his ear, "Elia, Elia, it's only the beginning, tomorrow evening we will reach even higher levels of ecstasy with Morgan. Our nectar burns with unfulfilled desires. Tonight, we will ignite our fantasies with the flames of our uninhibited lovemaking. As we free ourselves from the adolescent sexuality of the bourgeoisie world and their profane taboos."

I begin to strip Elia of his textile facade, revealing his tall thin well-formed frame – not frail, it is as aplomb as it is fluid, so like Elia's persona, an enigma and a contradiction. He is a gentleman, though uninhibited, seeking perfection and balance in an imperfect and unbalanced world.

"Seek and ye shall find," Elia muses to himself. "Are clichés aphrodisiacs as well?" He begins to massage Absinthe over Anais' naked body. "Her favorite drink, and now mine as well," he thinks to himself.

Elia takes off my bandana to blindfold me.

"Why professor, what are you hiding from me?"

"Anais, it is said that when one loses one of their senses, the other senses become more perceptive to compensate for the loss."

I chuckle and smile as I get down on my knees.

"Well then professor, I will have to taste what I can't see."

We enter the bath, teasing and tantalizing each other in preparation for Varikrida.[10]

"So, Elia, it must be true that cleanliness is next to holiness. Am I now holy Elia?"

"Let me kiss your divinity," Elia says with a seductive smile.

After completing our aqua erotic foreplay, we slowly towel each other off, all the while continuing to explore each other's intimate geography. We run naked through the loft to the kitchen to grab a bottle of Absinthe to use as a double aphrodisiac; to ingest and inflame our libidos as well as to use to massage each other again.

We surrender to each other as practitioners of the Kama Sutra. I prepare two glasses of Absinthe. First, I pour a few ounces in each glass, then placing the Absinthe spoon with perforated openings over the glass, I place a sugar cube on the spoon and pour some Absinthe over the cube. I light it with a match to melt into the Absinthe, then I pour a few ounces of water over the spoon.

Elia makes a toast to an evening of prolonged and experimental lovemaking. He embraces and kisses me as he gently strokes my skin. I am dressed in goose bumps. We find ourselves lying on one of the oriental rugs in the living area where we begin to make love again. We massage each other with Absinthe and lick ourselves into sexual intoxication.

We explore each other without restriction like two bodies sharing one passionate mind and genitalia, always knowing each

---

[10] "Making love in the water."

other's desires in advance, always ready to please.

I turn Elia on his back to straddle him. We face each other and engage in some dirty talk. Between the sheets of ecstasy, I reveal no lies or truths, only a suspension of my morality to satisfy my passions. I define my morality loosely so as not to encumber my new-found sexuality. I sigh with each Absinthe coated lick until we come together, sharing our nectar.

In our prolonged orchestrated sexual romp, we head back to the kitchen for another round of Absinthe to keep our libidos in overdrive. Elia seats me on the table, puts my back down and raises my legs. I rest my ankles on his shoulders and we engage in the Varahaghata[11]. Our lovemaking goes on until the early morning hours. We are too sexually intoxicated to count our orgasms.

We find ourselves embraced in the bedroom as we wake to a new golden dawn peering through the skylight. I rise to make coffee and a quick breakfast of yogurt and fresh fruit.

After breakfast, Elia heads to his quiet room for morning meditations, prayers, and invocations. He then goes to his library for solitary reading and writing. I head to the art gallery with one of his editions of the Kama Sutra. I stretch out on the new leather sofa and cuddle up with the book. I throw a blanket over myself for shelter from the loft's cold spots, a byproduct of the multi-floor clearstory interior design with massive floor-to-ceiling windows. I read each page, examining the photos with curiosity and anticipation. I want to learn more about this form of lovemaking that Elia has embraced. I am also looking for inspiration to be creative with Morgan who seems quite comfortable and confident with her bisexuality as I am trying to come to terms with my own sexuality.

---

[11] "Boar's thrust."

Morgan is a sensual woman who respects her partners and does not see sex as a competition – purely synergy – always making the best possible experience for all involved. Her agenda is always true, though her motives are always suspect. I feel confident and happy that my plan has worked out so well. I have Ben to thank for this. I not quite sure how Elia and Morgan will react to my plan. As I thumb through the pages, I pat myself for pulling off such a coup, and fill my bucket list with another fait accompli.

In my solitude I have some time to reflect on the emotional conundrum I must face, one I did not plan on, and one I fear to navigate. My bucket-list plan was simply to find a sex partner without any emotional encumbrances and to fulfill my long-denied desires and fantasies before surrendering to gravity and menopause. I believe a few good memories are better than a life of regrets. I have been pressured by the fear of knowing mortality is finite with an unknown expiration date.

Am I wrong to believe this? To think otherwise would render me a fool and a moralist who believes in an eternal soul. Elia is no fool and I admire his Gnostic spiritual morality, which at times I feel is in conflict with my own agnostic beliefs. Well, maybe I should not give it too much thought, and "not put off till tomorrow what I can do today" with Elia and Morgan. Ha, ha, clichés. Though I have to admit I live by them, they are the psalms of my agnostic bible and Aphrodite is my patron saint.

I continue to amuse myself with my quick wit as I turn the pages of the Kama Sutra. With delight I project Elia, Morgan, and myself into the photographs. I am getting sexually aroused as I view the lovers entwined in their sexual positions. I sigh. Luckily, we are all practitioners of yoga, so we can contort our bodies into these pleasurable lovemaking positions. "No pain, no gain," – clichés.

I have to face the reality that I am developing strong emotional feelings for Elia, feelings I have never felt for any man. I enjoy his company, the dinners, the intellectual talks, his humble sophistication, and his spiritualized lovemaking, which I find engaging and enjoyable. I think of him when I am not with him, when he is working, teaching, or at Masonic lodge meetings. I want to spend more time with him, but I have to deal with some serious soul searching that I am not prepared for.

I admire Elia's depth of honesty, as much as I fear it. Elia never hides behind his subconscious mind, for his subconscious and conscious minds are one. Truth and transparency are the core of his ethics and morality – no double standards. He cuts himself little to no slack in his morality and leaves no stone unturned in his search for truth, or when faced with a moral enigma. If he finds a shred of hypocrisy within himself, he is the first to cast a stone. Elia had reservations about this evening's ménage-a-trois with Morgan. In his honesty he readily admitted it was a fantasy he has, though he questions his own character for having created a fantasy with so much power. He questions his own rationale of the duality of flesh and soul and if he is giving far too much credence to the flesh at the expense of the soul. Elia cannot lie to himself, or to anyone for that matter. Though he will admit the ménage-a-trois will bring him to the heights of his sexual ecstasy, when I asked him if he felt it would be a liberating experience, he responded with painful honesty that often we project a false definition into the word liberate to satisfy our own agenda. We can become trapped if we are not honest with ourselves or if we are in denial of our fears, he had said. He gave the example of a student liberating himself from the demands of studying for good academic standing by partying only to fail in his studies. Yes, the student had liberated himself, but we should ask if the student bettered himself. If we define liberation as the abandonment of responsibility, we have reduced it to our prison of fears and self-doubt. Elia is the consummate existentialist.

In an attempt to quell my brain virus, I walk over to Elia's library. The door is open, and Elia is still deep into his meditations. I peruse his voluminous library with the hope of finding a book that will offer the words to appease my existential epiphany. Elia has an extensive collection of existential books. As I eye the shelves, I am drawn to Simone de Beauvoir's book, *The Second Sex*. Either by chance, or an act of synchronicity, I open the book to the chapter addressing her feelings. I am not given the answer I am looking for, though reading the chapter has made me see I am not alone in my thinking and emotions. Yes, I think with an impish smile, "Many women find themselves intimidated by a prestigious morality, though many of us know we are unable to conform with it inwardly. Ironically, we respect the law we are breaking, and we suffer for our crimes. We suffer more for having found accomplices."

I gently return the book to its place and drift back into my sexual daydream. I see myself naked in bed on satin sheets between Morgan and Elia. Their soft and probing hands take liberty with my welcoming body. In my mind, I begin to plan the evening's sexual carnival, then with a sigh, I decide I will leave it to fate. I have the strength and confidence to play the role of the submissive, knowing in reality I will be the one in control of the ménage-a-trios. I also know Elia and Morgan will perform the fantasies we want to transmute into our realities without offering commands or requests. Losing track of the time, I continue to turn the pages of the Kama Sutra with desire and glee as I project myself into the photographs again to pleasure my imagination.

My fantasy is broken when Elia enters the gallery.

"Anais, it's 2:00 p.m. Morgan is expected to arrive around 6:00- 6:30. We need to get the loft in order, pick up a few things, and you need to stop at home to check on your daughters and change your clothes."

Pulled from my reverie, I go to the bathroom, shower, dress, and head out on my errands.

I return around 5:30 dressed in my Boho best, carrying a few packages and an overnight bag. Elia greets me at the door and grabs the packages. I pour us each a glass of wine and make a toast.

"To our shared infidelity."

We clink glasses and kiss.

"So, Elia, are you as excited about our first ménage-a-trois as I am?"

"Excited as I am curious."

"Elia, did you ever think when we met at Karen's Demitasse Café life would take us down this path?"

"I see it as more of an adventure, let's not compromise the essence of our story."

"Well, I am sure you will like Morgan's company on many levels. She is genuine with a good heart. A woman with her looks and position could be far haughtier and more self-centered than she is. She knows how to rise above herself. This is why I think we will make such a good ménage-a-trois. Well, she should be here any minute now."

Trilingus

*"How shall we account for the captivating
power and mystery of feminine existence?"*
–Soren Kierkegaard

Morgan arrives on time as expected. She is obsessive about being on time. She is traveling light with only an overnight bag and a few bottles of wine as a housewarming gift.

Anais greets Morgan at the door, noticing that Elia's eyes are quick to take note of her beauty and grace. Anais feels the instant chemistry that ignites between them, which makes her a bit threatened and jealous. Then she muses, "How can I think this way? After this evening we will be each-other's whore and master, each other's fantasy." She congratulates herself on her brinksmanship having pulled this off. Then silently laughs with glee. "I have beaten Ben at his own game."

Elia quickly takes note that Morgan, like Anais, is wearing the best chic boho money can buy. She even looks like Anais in many ways. They are about the same height; same color hair, though Morgan's hair is a bit longer and wilder, and they both have the same body frame. Also, like Anais, Morgan has well-proportioned angular facial features that are accented by her aviator sunglasses. She looks to be in her mid-thirties and very WASPish with a hybrid sophisticated/artist's swag. Her attitude is artsy and free of much intellectualism. She is beautiful, enticing, and welcoming, complete with a few danger signs.

Elia takes Morgan's bag and the bottles of wine as Anais and Morgan caress and kiss. Then, with arms around each other, Anais formally introduces Morgan to Elia. Morgan initiates a hug and passionate kiss.

"So nice to meet you Elia, you have a really nice loft. Anais speaks so highly of you. Though I would now have to say, having met you in person, your persona is much more dynamic and charismatic. I look forward to getting to know you better and intimately. Anais and I do not kiss and tell."

"Thank you, Morgan, your words are very kind, and Anais has spoken equally well of you, though words could never capture your radiant animation. I am sure we all share a common bond as artists and romantics, seeking our sensual essence of life."

"Well Elia, since our diner reservation is at 7:00 at our favorite Thai Restaurant just across the street, I will give Morgan a tour of your loft."

Anais and Morgan head toward the gallery hand-in-hand, each holding a glass of wine. Elia goes to his study to make a few last-minute business calls.

Morgan makes some private mental notes on Elia's design as she walks the three levels of the loft and the open balcony overlooking the main reception hall. Morgan, like Anais, finds Elia's design naked and raw, exposing his soul and his search for truth. She is drawn to its mystical call as it speaks to her soul, though she is afraid to answer. Morgan has become intrigued with Elia and wants to get into his head. She too is confused. For a man who reveals himself, he still holds a mystery; even to himself.

Elia has reserved his favorite table at the Thai restaurant. It is located in a quiet corner by a window overlooking the autumn street scape with its bare trees standing ready to embrace winter, their orphaned rainbow leaves fluttering in an evening's breeze. On the sidewalk lovers stroll hand-in-hand under a full bright moon.

Being a patron of the Kama Sutra, Elia knows the dinner is intended to act as the evening's foreplay, affording him the opportunity to get closer to Morgan.

Once inside the restaurant he notices her bright hazel eyes, full of life and passion. The restaurant, as always, is crowded, prompting Morgan to comment, "Good pick Elia, the crowd speaks for itself. The restaurant also has the highest Zagat rating. What do you suggest for starters?"

"We are all romantics, and romance begins with the taste buds," Elia says. He orders a dozen oysters on the half-shell, Tom Kha Gai, and Yum Nuea. "This will keep our dinner light and spicy to arouse our Kundalini serpent power this evening."

Morgan smiles at Anais, then Elia.

"Elia, are you speaking from experience or theory?"

"Well Morgan, I can't think of a better time to put the theory into practice."

Anais chimes in, "Well, we will have to order seconds to validate the theory." Her interjection is an ice breaker that opens up the conversation to more intimate talk.

Morgan raises her glass. "To Anais, congratulations on getting the role in your first nude indie film."

Anais is quite surprised. "Morgan! How did this happen? I thought for sure Ben would interfere and ruin it for me."

"Anais, believe me, I know how to handle Ben. Like all animals, to train them all you have to do is feed them."

Elia turns to Anais and kisses her. "Congratulations!"

Morgan sensing that everyone is becoming more comfortable with each other, interjects, "So Elia, how are you going to explain to your clients, office staff, and the business community that your partner will be starring in an indie film complete with a nude lesbian sex scene?"

"Well Morgan, what's the problem? I'm an architect and

artist, a true man of aesthetics. I follow the design principle that all form follows function, and as architects say, when it comes to design, less is more."

Anais and Morgan respond with laughter. "I told you. Elia has an answer for everything," Anais quips.

After appetizers they order an entrée of vegetable Pad Thai to share and another round of red wine.

"So, Elia the consummate existentialist, here I am getting ready for our grand ménage-a-trois. With you and Anais in a relationship, and Anais and I having had an affair prior to your relationship, you are now going to make love to me while making love to Anais at the same time. And I am going to make love to you for the first time with Anais. Is this what existentialists refer to as the absurdity of life?"

Elia pauses for a moment as he smiles his Cheshire cat grin.

"Yes. It's one of those rare and fortunate absurdities we are most grateful for. As we say in Italian, *non c'è due senza tre,* there is no two with three, three is the perfect number."

Morgan lets out a laugh, then moves her hand under the table to place it on Elia's sex, only to find that Anais already has squatter's rights. She settles for his thigh and continues to laugh.

The banter continues.

"So, Elia, do you think this evening's ménage-a-trois will influence your architecture in any way?" Morgan asks.

Elia smiles and pauses to collect his thoughts. "Well, I am one who appreciates the divine proportion so well manifested on such beautiful women as you and Anais. Yes, I can see my designs transition from a more angular geometry to a more fluid geometry emphasizing curves."

Morgan appreciates Elia's quick wit. "Well then, I look forward to seeing your next designs. What do you say we pass on the dessert and head back to the loft? I am eager to offer you some architectural inspiration for your next project."

Back at the loft Anais prepares the Absinthe to set the mood for the ménage-à-trois. Elia lights sandalwood incense in the bedroom and hits 'play' on a selection of sensual new age music.

Morgan undresses. "Elia, can you point me in the direction of the shower?"

Soon Anais and Elia join Morgan. Elia embraces her from behind as he whispers in her ear, "The Kama Sutra teaches bathing is the best way to begin lovemaking. It allows our bodies to touch with affection and slowly arouses our passions.

Their shower foreplay is the appetizer that whets their passions for the evening's sexual banquet. They wash each other slowly sharing tender kisses. They squeeze their bodies together and against the wet marble walls as the water jets wash away any lingering inhibitions.

They exit the shower and slowly towel each other off to increase the sensations of their arousal. They run to Elia's bedroom and fall upon his king-size bed. The lavender-scented white satin sheets have already been pulled back. They begin to massage each other from head to toe with sandalwood, musk, Ylang Ylang, and bergamot oils.

Elia prepares three glasses of Absinthe, which they sip, then rub on each other. They nibble and nuzzle under the moon-lit skylight, looking up at the stars and at each other. They are delighting in each other's bodies, minds, and souls, stirring all the sensations of their senses to awaken their serpent Kundalini power. They gently kiss and explore with soft intimacies like virgins having their first sexual experience.

They whisper secret shibboleths to each other under the satin canopy as they giggle with delight when their hands find each other's sex. They are hypnotized, having reached a higher state of consciousness brought on by orchestrated sexual ecstasy.

"I am enjoying our trilingus and feel comfortable and secure making love to Morgan and Elia," Anais thinks. "We find ourselves not competing for one another's lust but have become a sexual ensemble, finely tuned and never missing a beat."

"We are like pilgrims in the night finding our spiritual awakening, not an emotionless orgy satisfied with mere goop releases," Elia ponders. "We hold each other with the twine of sexual bondage. We are three people living in one skin experiencing multiple synchronized orgasms climaxing in three-part harmony."

"While making love to Anais and Morgan, the three-ring circus is silent in my head. That circus masks my childhood abuse at the hands of my father, along with all the mocking insults from my mother. For the first time in my life, I feel a physical and spiritual presence of peace and love enter my beingness, one that has been denied me since birth. All my years of giving love were never returned, until now as I lay with Morgan and Anais. Free and removed from the profane world of hate and greed, for each kiss and touch of love is returned twofold. In these intimate moments my mind is free from itself. I feel a clear river rushing through my soul purifying me and removing the barnacles of dross that have pained me throughout life. I feel I am now one with the sacred eternal river as it takes me to my long-awaited heaven, away from this alien land."

In their sexual frenzy they run about the loft from room to room to make love. They are immune to the drafts that cover their naked bodies in goose bumps. They frolic about like children with the benefit of mature sexuality.

Anais and Morgan run up the stairs arm-in-arm kissing and caressing each other. Then they call out for Elia when they reach the top floor. He joins them and they collapse on one of the oriental carpets. Morgan shouts out, feeling the effects of the

Absinthe, "All for one, one for all," as she snuggles her way in between Anais and Elia. They laugh licking the Absinthe off of each other. Around 3:00 a.m. they fall asleep in the arms of Morpheus.

"I am pleasantly surprised and satisfied with Anais and Elia's expanding sexual acumen, and their rapid learning curve, especially being ménage-à-trois virgins," Morgan considers before falling asleep.

"Our creativity and passions are our sex toys. We share the same balance and timing. We are three sexualists dancing in perfect step to the three-quarter time of a waltz that triggers our mutual and numerous orgasms. I feel a sexual synergy with Anais and Elia, and a real physical and emotional connection with Elia that disturbs me as it challenges me. I feared I would want to get closer to him at Anais' expense. How long can this sexual trilingus endure before turning ugly?"

Sunday Morning

I wake to a golden dawn laid out on my bed between Anais and Morgan. They are asleep. I do not wake them. I rise to shave and shower. Alone, staring into the bathroom mirror, I begin to second guess last evening's sexual libertine romp, questioning why I had agreed to it. My mind engages in an existential conflict between physical bliss and my Gnostic spiritual restraint. Is it just cause and effect? Synchronicity? A dream come-true? Where will this take me? How will it end? My mind drifts to my reading of *Lord of the Flies* as I juxtapose the moral of the story onto last evening's crash into a sexual jungle free of institutional sexual restraints and taboos. How easy our morals fall when we are set free from our inhibitions and social restraints. I pull myself from my nauseating existential tailspin. Maybe it's simply a case of *in compagnia pres moglie un frate*[12]. A simple word of wisdom, not a cliché. Well, no one is listening. I laugh at myself in the mirror.

Anais joins me. Morgan, who has done her morning yoga in the nude in the gallery, also enters the bathroom. We shower together to reinvigorate ourselves from our exhaustive sexual gymnastics. Morgan is quick to shower and dress. She leaves to return to the gallery. Anais and I tarry in the shower.

We look at ourselves in one of the shower mirrors. Anais is picking through her hair. "Dam, Elia," she says with concern. "A few more grey hairs. I'm getting old! Father Time is at my heels.

---

[12] Sometimes the company of certain people can make us do things that we would otherwise never do.

125

He does not play fair. Life is not fair. How little time do I have before I turn into an old crone?"

"Anais, we all grow old if we are lucky, though you will never grow into a crone." I towel-dry her and wrap a large towel around her. I mutter under my breath, *a pagare emorir c ē sempre tempo*[13].

As Anais leaves to dress, I take another look at myself. Yes, there are a few grey hairs and the beginning of frown and marionette lines that come with aging. This does not bother me. I am not vain and have known since taking my first steps in life that I am walking to my death at some unknown date in the future.

I again begin to muse. "I have just lived the ultimate male fantasy and should be drunk with my conquest. If I were like Sal, I would be at a bar surrounded by drunken guys boasting with bragging rights about my sexual conquest. I am a gentleman and respect my partners and my own sexual privacy. I will never lower myself to the level of the profane or become a cafone like Sal. Lovemaking is an art not to be desecrated, nor is it to be displayed in a gallery of voyeurs.

As Elia dresses and Anais makes breakfast, Morgan heads up to the gallery and plops down on the leather couch to reflect on last evening's ménage-à-trois.

"A grand journal for sure!" she says to herself. "It was so pure, genuine, and spontaneous. There was no need for my director skills, we were in perfect balance. And I amused myself with my own banter. Too bad we didn't film it.

"The experience was just me playing the part of the avant-garde director/artist following the job description and accepted behavior for running with the bohemian herd. I'm a hedonist at

---

[13] No rush to pay or die.

heart living each day seeking the satisfaction of my changing desires, a sexual chameleon for sure. Lovemaking is for the flesh. Emotions and love itself are hindrances and constructs. At best, they are the possessions of the weak to be easily exploited for one's advantage. Fulfilled desire trumps friendship, trust, and fidelity. I disdain trust and fidelity more than Elia disdains clichés. I'm a sexualist and opportunist. And I am honest enough with myself to know this. I just have no room in my life for sincerity."

Morgan heads down to the kitchen to catch up with Elia and Anais, and to grab a quick cup of coffee before heading out.

"Thanks Anais and Elia for quite an enchanting evening to say the least. A beautiful memory for sure. Don't worry, I promise, I won't kiss and tell. I have to run to the city for a film shoot, so let's try to hook up in a few weeks and do it again. I really like hanging out in this loft."

Morgan gives Anais a big hug and kiss and heads out. Anais closes the door to the loft behind Morgan and sighs. She walks over to Elia and cuddles in his arms feeling a bit insecure and confused. Silently she ponders her mixed emotions.

"I feel an inner anguish knowing I am developing strong emotional feelings for Elia. This is something I never counted on. My plan was simply to find a charming and interesting man to have an affair with. Now I find myself drawn to Elia more and more each day, wanting to know more about him, wanting to get inside his head as he has gotten into mine. I have never before been drawn to a man as I am to Elia. He is different, he is an outlier, genuine and honest. I am an agnostic, but I am drawn to his Gnostic spiritualism and mysticism, though I hardly understand it. My unbelieving ways are being washed away like fine sands on an outgoing tide. It calls me, it calms me, and brings me peace, though I fear it. I sometimes feel I have taken my dream to its limits, only to wake in my own nightmare of regrets."

Anais excuses herself and heads to the bedroom to get some much-needed sleep. Elia heads to his gallery.

Anais catches up with Elia in the afternoon. He is still in the gallery working on a few pen and ink sketches, obviously caught up in another one of his increasingly frequent mind-walks.

"Elia, you know, I can actually hear you think."

"Well Anais, you're not the first person to tell me this. So, what am I thinking?"

"Elia, why do you over-think everything?"

"Ha! Because I can't afford to under-think."

"O hell Elia. Does your fucking analytical cerebral mind ever rest?"

"Sure, between each thought."

"Dam you Elia, do you always have to have an answer for everything?"

"As long as you have questions for me."

"Ahh Elia, so share with me your thoughts about art, you never mention your sketches, and you never told me about your art exhibitions."

"I just dabble. It's a diversion to help reduce stress."

"And what about your poetry?"

"Ahh Anais, merely another color on my artist's palette to highlight existence."

"So, Elia, share your thoughts with me on this. I am curious to know more about the complexity of your never-sleeping mind."

"O Anais, now you are going to place my professor's hat on my head. This can be sterile talk for some ears."

"Elia, you forget, I'm also an artist, I will cast no stones upon you for your refinements like your ex-wife and daughters."

"Anais, to be true artists our work must be objective and aim for a specific impression. Therefore, it cannot be subjective. We must know beforehand what we want to convey and do it with clarity, so it leaves the same impression on all who view it – like a mathematical calculation. We must know our target and never miss our mark. Our art must be able to emotionally transmit knowledge to a level beyond our intellect. The Orientals believe art is a finger pointing at the moon. Regretfully, today we have prostituted art by mistaking the finger for the moon."

A loud knocking sounds on the secondary entrance door. Anais goes to attend it.

"Good morning Christine and Sarah, please come in. I'll call your father."

The girls walk in with attitude and stand ignoring Anais as Elia approaches.

"Good Morning Christine and Sarah, would you like some Demitasse, fresh fruit and yogurt, or maybe some strawberries and cream for breakfast?"

Christine looks at Sarah. "Oooohhh, Sarah, would you like some Demitasse and some strawberries and crème? Ha, ha, ha, isn't dad such a fucking fagot?"

"So, what brings you here this morning?" Elia asks.

Christine answers, "Well my car broke down and I need some money to get it fixed."

"I see, is this something Sal can fix? I understand he is good with fixing cars, am I correct?"

"Well, he's working today."

"Well girls, how can that be? It's Sunday and the job site is closed. Before I forget, I have a few things you left behind on your last visit. Wait here, I'll get them for you."

Elia returns with Christine's guitar and Sarah's scholarship for art class.

Elia hands them their gifts. "Here girls, I believe you forgot to take these the last time you were here."

Sarah takes the envelope, rips it up and throws it on the floor.

"Fuck you Dad, I told you I don't want this stupid white-collar uppity gift!"

Christine opens the guitar case. "What the fuck kind of stupid gift is this – a Martin guitar? She slams it against one of the columns breaking it into pieces. Take your fucking fagot artsy gift. Mom and Sal said these are useless. Now where is my check so I can get my car fixed, Dad!"

"Excuse me while I get my checkbook."

Anais looks at Elia with horror and rage as he walks off, then returns.

"So, girls, how much will it cost to repair your car?"

"O say, about $1,500."

"I see and what is wrong with the car?"

Sarah answers, "Sal says it needs a new transmission."

"So soon? The car is only a few years old."

"Dad, don't dispute Sal, he knows what he is talking about."

"Well girls do you really trust him?"

"More than we trust a lying white-collar loser like you."

"I see."

Anais cringes as Elia writes out a check. He starts to hand it to the girls, then rips it up and throws it on the floor.

"I am sure, Christine and Sarah, that you would feel bad taking money from a white-collar professional loser. It's best you go seek help from your idol Sal."

They both start stamping their feet.

"I want my money! You owe it to us. Fuck you dad! This only proves that Sal is the better man."

"Well girls, I suggest you go talk to his ex-wife. I'm not paying his back alimony payments. Do you take me to be a fool?

Now, please, leave. I'm sure you can find your way out. *L'occasione fa l'uomo ladra.*[14]"

"So, Dad, what are you saying about Sallie?"

"Sarah, be wise enough to know opportunity makes the thief."

---

[14] Every opportunity not taken is lost.

The Orphaned Father

After Elia's daughters leave, I embrace him to console him. He is unmoved like an ancient stoic – his emotions like a rock.

"Elia, I really don't want to intrude, but I just can't stand by and watch your daughters disrespect you and try to manipulate you. Can't you try to talk to them and get them to see what white trash Sallie is?"

This is the first time I've seen Elia short on words. He pauses and takes a deep breath, then mumbles under his breath, *quando la neve si scioglie si scopre la mondezza.*

"Elia please! English!"

"Sorry, I'm just in one of my cerebral mind walks. I said, 'when the snow melts, the trash is revealed.'"

"Elia, do you think your daughters will ever learn?"

"There are none so dear as those who do not want to hear."

"Elia, now I'm really starting to worry about you, another cliché?"

"No, just a proverb. Proverbs are for the wise, clichés are for fools and the profane."

"You always have an answer, I would hate to have you as my professor."

I smile as I try to unwind Elia, and to get him back to his charming self.

"So, Elia, how do you reconcile this with your existential Gnostic mind? I need to hear this, to know how you can be so unmoved by this?"

"My daughters, like so many people, make their projections as perception. As they think, so they perceive. They fail to see and understand perception is not the result, but the cause. With this said, it's a better path to not try to change the world, but to change your mind about the world. The mortal world is a self-induced illusion. If we accept this illusion, we are delusional."

"Elia, it's the perfect fall day, let's take a walk along the river to wind down from last night's sexual high. We can stop at one of the restaurants along the river for a drink to celebrate our new-found sexuality. Who said three's a crowd? Sorry Elia, I just had to throw that in at your expense, and besides, I can't disguise it in French."

Elia takes my hand, and we walk out of the loft. We find a nice spot to sit alfresco. As we sip our wine, I continue my inquiry to get a better understanding of Elia's existential and Gnostic philosophies. Over the past weeks we have shared so much of our intimacies, but I am now sincerely interested in knowing and understanding his interior spiritual soul. He often refers to it in passing, without much commentary. It shows up as another scribble from his mind, saying, "I am here. This is me. This is why I exist."

I am beginning to also feel my soul, which I long denied as a border-line agnostic/atheist. I was raised as an Episcopalian, though abandoned any faith after meeting Ben. I now also feel I have been distancing myself from Ben both physically and spiritually. The only thing Ben worships is himself, fueled by his self-directed egotistic choir. In Ben's parlance, if you can't touch it and derive pleasure from it, it's not worth a second thought.

"So, Elia, please understand. I'm not prying or trying to undermine you. I just need to know more about you. Your world arouses my curiosity. I want to know your soul as well as your flesh. You are still an enigma to me, as I am a neophyte in your world."

Elia looks a little uncertain and perplexed.

"Anais, you are not prying, for these are not trying questions. Though, this is the first time I have heard you mention anything about your soul. I guard my beliefs jealousy."

"Out of fear or ridicule? Don't worry Elia, this is not a witch hunt. I would like you to share this with me. I want to learn."

"Anais, please understand, Gnostics are not evangelists. Our beliefs are manifested by the actions of our souls."

"Elia, is this why you so much engage life and live it to the fullest as a renaissance man and intellectual? Or is it all merely a diversion from the disrespect you receive from your ex and daughters?"

"My beliefs provide me with the wisdom to not to let my ex and daughters, and the profane world, manipulate my soul and harm me. I will not concede this power to them – it's evil."

"So then, why are you so obsessed with creating architecture, art, and writings that will outlive you while you believe in the immortality of the soul? I'm not debating you, Elia, I just have a strong yearning to know. It will help guide me to my transition."

"Regardless of other's actions and knowing that other people can be hell, I rise above man-made and self-inflicted misery. My soul won't allow me to contract this contagious illness. There is a philosophical saying, 'Mortals die three deaths; our passing, our burial, and the last time our name is mentioned.'"

"Why then do you worry when you believe in a heaven and immortality of the soul?"

"With a grain of salt, I amuse myself knowing my ex and daughters will continue using my name well after I'm gone for good or bad. Anais, we must mark our days well in life by leaving honorable footprints behind for people to follow in the hope of straightening out the crooked timber of humanity. For each footprint followed, we will be remembered. Good deeds can be as contagious as gossip. What we choose to listen to renders us divine or profane."

"Elia, excuse my comment and please take it as a compliment. I doubt your children will ever be able to navigate your footsteps and will always keep your name alive with insults as long as they follow in Sal's serpentine path of stupidity."

"Anais, I find consolation in knowing it is better to be an orphaned father by alienation from my daughters, rather than by loss of my daughters. In their life, is my hope."

A Wing and a Prayer

Today is the opening and dedication of the Behavioral Health wing at Saint Dymphna's Hospital. Elia designed and dedicated the new wing in honor of his uncle – a project he has aspired to since he was a teenager. Not only is it an emotional day for Elia it marks a well-earned professional achievement as well.

The press and local dignitaries are present for the photoshoot and post-dedication reception. Elia talks to the attentive crowd and well-wishers in his usual confident and articulate manner, though he is a bit self-effacing. Although Elia is a master of hiding his emotions behind a stoic and confident façade, I do feel his uneasiness as he gives his presentation and mingles with the guests. Elia respects social protocols, though he has a distain for arrogance and vain showmanship.

Elia introduces me to his long-time friends Saint Dymphna's CEO, Steve Carroll, who was instrumental in dedicating the addition in Elia's uncle's honor and Monsignor Chad Donohue, who Elia has known since his teen years when he attended Saint Camillis DeLellis high school where the Monsignor was principal.

To quell any rumors, I am attending as Elia's guest, sitting at his side as the photographer to cover the event for Elia's portfolio. The local newspaper also takes a photograph for the front page of the next day's edition that includes all the dignitaries and Elia with his arm around me. Subtle as it is, it catches the presses eye as well as the guests and dignitaries – front page news for sure.

The reception is held at the posh Hudson Shore Yacht Club.

The guest list includes the benefactors, politicians, doctors, media, clergy, Elia's key staff including Liz, the contractor, the hospital's management team, and board of directors.

I am seated next to Elia at the head table along with the CEO, Monsignor, the Contractor, the Mayor, and Senator. Each makes a brief presentation thanking the others for their contributions, stressing the need for more behavioral healthcare facilities in the Hudson Valley. I do not give a talk for obvious reasons. Liz, Elia's office manager, is also present and she shares the story of Elia burning the midnight oil to personally work on the design to keep costs at a minimum.

My feelings about attending this function are bitter-sweet. I am so happy for Elia and honored to be with him on his day of achievement and recognition. I am also glad he did not have to attend another celebration alone, though I feel equally uncomfortable about the cold shoulder I receive all during the event from Liz and other members of his staff in attendance. They view me as some form of interloper. Is Liz just jealous and protective? I have to respect this. I would not act differently if I were in her shoes.

I am truly happy for Elia and feel I have been a good influence for him. I enjoy his company and spending as much time with him as my responsibilities as a mother allow. I know Elia to be a unique outlier intellectually and spiritually. He has keen perception and heightened emotional intelligence. With all these qualities and his charming and positive character, it's easy to see why he is well known and liked, though it seems he is never truly understood and appreciated by those who know him. Elia lives in the moment though he is never present. I always feel the loneliness and alienation that permeates his soul as well as his art and architecture. It's a woman's intuition, I guess. O hell, another one of those dam clichés Elia has such disdain for. A true heart never lies, regardless of the pain.

I interrupt my silent mental reverie to rejoin the festive party. There is live music and dancing, and the hall is decorated in the full-bloom of the fast-approaching holiday season. The event affords Elia time to spend with his friend and confidant Steve Carroll, and to do some business networking.

Elia and I decide to leave before the band commences the dancing and in order to deny the paparazzi and the rumor mill from compromising Elia's achievement. We stay long enough to satisfy the protocols of social etiquette and graces, though we leave early enough to avoid the lingering crowd that would probe and disrespect our privacy. I know full well, if we stay longer Elia's achievement and humanitarian work will take second place to rumors and gossip.

I decide to stay over at Elia's for the night so we can finalize arrangements for our vacation to Martinique in two weeks. I am looking forward to spending some time away from my daughters and Ben. And I look forward to spending unbroken time with Elia partying in the Caribbean.

After a nightcap Elia and I shower together to engage in some aqua erotica. As I am caught up in our lovemaking, which is getting more intense with each orgasm and broken taboo, I feel I am redlining my sexual libido without a destination, running on emotions well-past half empty. It does not matter to me. I am living in the moment, living my essence, filling my sexual bucket list, and emptying my closet of future regrets. Fools dream of a better tomorrow; wise men live a better tomorrow in the present, yet the future does not exist since it has not arrived.

I oversleep, waking mid-morning. Elia has already left to teach an early class at one of the local colleges. I have no plans for the day, so I just tarry at Elia's. I head over to Elia's library, his sacred ground. He has left the library door open and unlocked – this is so unlike him. My curiosity gets the better of me. I walk in and notice a number of open books, many with page markers, on the center table. A closer look reveals they are books on Gnosticism, existential philosophy, and Free Masonry. These topics are of little interest to me, though I take a casual perusal of the contents to get a better understanding of Elia's mind and soul. There is also a hand-scripted poem on the table. I take the liberty to read it.

Elia's Journal | December 5, 1992 | 3:00 a.m.

Astarte's Fall
O beautiful earth mother, blessed Astarte
Where art thou lover Adonis?
Has he left you barren?
And, alone in autumn's death throes?
For now, the brilliant sun retires with Adonis,
Who now sleeps with Persephone.

O earth mother, your once radiant tides
Now turn to cold tears that freeze nature in your womb
While your lover hides
Fields lay fallow in the melancholy of raptures loss.

O mother of earth
Cold winds now fall below your once majestic trees
Once a cornucopia of summer's bounty
Now a victim of winter's grip
A lover's loss that now renders your beauty
A cold and contorted landscape.

Leaves fall from dead trees
A reflection upon the misfortunes of lost loves
For each fallen leaf is a memory of summer's past love
O jilted lover
Winter is your scorn upon the earth
Till your lover Adonis warms your womb
With his kiss of spring.

Only Smiles and Sun Block

Anais and Elia head to their romantic getaway in Martinique. It is another of Anais' first-time surprise bucket-list adventures for an unsuspecting Elia.

As they are chauffeured from the airport to their private resort, Anais smiles devilishly at Elia.

"Elia, looks like you have over-packed. We are heading to a beach resort, not a country club. You know what the natives say in this part of the island?"

"Well, you got me Anais, what do the natives say?"

Anais laughs disarmingly. "Well Elia, where we are going the dress code is simply 'only smiles and sunscreen'. Capiche? Elia."

Elia returns her question with an ear-to-ear smile. "Capiche, Anais. As we architects like to say, 'less is more'."

"So, Elia, I take it you're not the inhibited type."

"Anais, we are artists, we have to be expressive. As artists we cannot be expressive if we are inhibited now, can we?"

"Well, I should have expected an answer like this from you."

"So, Anais, aside from your new movie, have you ever gone au natural in public or skinny dipping before?"

Anais pauses for a moment. "Sure Elia, in college I did life modeling for art classes to earn extra money. It was a real easy gig. Not a bad gig at all. And you Elia?"

Elia's mind flashes back to one summer evening when he had just purchased his home and had the in-ground pool installed. He had arrived home quite late, around 11:00ish from a client meeting in Westchester. The girls were out at a slumber party and Beth was home alone. It was very hot and humid, and Elia was wearing a formal suit. When he entered the house, it was dark. He went to the back of the house where he saw Beth sitting in a lounge chair wearing a modest two-piece bathing suit that exposed her well-formed body. She had recently dyed her hair blonde and was sipping white wine.

"Hey Beth, ready for a dip?"

"Not really," Beth said as she turned around.

Elia then stripped down to his skin and jumped in.

"Are you sure Beth? The water is warm. Come and join me for a dip."

Beth was unmoved.

"Hey Beth, are you just going to sit there and sweat in this heat? Come and join me. Throw off your bathing suit and let's have fun."

"Elia, Elia, the neighbors might see us."

"Beth, I designed this pool with privacy in mind. It's surrounded with a high wood-fence and full-coverage landscaping. There is a gazebo at one end, the back of the property is bounded by wetlands, and there is an elevated deck for the band when we throw our frequent parties. Besides, look. All the neighbors' lights are out. A little romance and spontaneity won't kill you. Let's have some fun while we can."

Beth took a few sips of wine, got up from the lounge chair and entered the pool. Elia went over and gave her a kiss and hug.

"Now Beth, are you going to take that bathing suit off or am I going to have to pull it off you?"

Beth smiled, took a few steps back, bent over in the water and came up with the bottom of her bathing suit in her hand. She threw it in the air.

"Now that's more like it, Beth."

Elia dove to caress Beth's ass and kiss her below the water

line. He emerged from the water, started kissing her and then took off her top. He threw it in the air, as they embraced and grinded against each other's sex. Their sex play took them to the upper deck, the gazebo, back into the pool, and finally the lower deck as they entertained all possibilities. They exhausted themselves to the point of falling asleep on the deck, awakening at dawn in a caress. Elia was quite surprised at Beth's playfulness and experimental sexuality. He began to believe she was starting to outgrow her insecurities and inhibitions.

The following day Elia felt the need to do something special for Beth, so he took her shopping for new living room and dining room furniture. Elia knew Beth was very self-conscious of her upbringing. She came from a hard-working and honest family of very limited means. She would lament how her parents always had to buy second-hand furniture or accept hand-me-downs. The furniture they already had was in very good shape and of good quality but did not suit the layout of the new house.

Once inside the pricey showroom, one that Beth had never stepped into before, Elia noticed her face light up like a child on Christmas morning. This moved Elia deeply as he remembered Beth's stories of waking up on Christmas day to few or no gifts. He wanted to correct this injustice.

Elia introduced, Jill, the interior designer, to Beth and gave them a floor plan of the house. He suggested they select furniture and get a quote. Elia had told Beth before they left that they were only doing window shopping since Elia would not have the funds to purchase the furniture until a few more commissions came in. Elia found much joy in watching Beth with her childlike smile walk around the showroom with the designer. He knew Beth was out of her element in the upscale showroom, so he had paid Jill in advance to take good care of Beth.

An hour or so later they returned with a sketched-out furniture plan, along with the price quote. Elia asked Beth if she liked what Jill had selected. Once again, Beth's face lit up like a candle. Jill handed Elia the quote.

"So, Elia, can we afford it? It's beautiful. I've never had anything like this in my entire life. Can you buy it for me?"

Elia's heart went out to Beth's plea. He winked at Jill.

"Wow, is this the best you can do with the price? Did you factor in my architect's discount?"

"Yes, of course Elia."

"Well to be honest I was not expecting to shell out this kind of money at this time."

"So, what should I do Elia?"

"Well, can you give me until Tuesday to get back to you and place a hold on the pieces?"

"You are asking a bit much, but for you Elia, I will do it, and no later than Tuesday."

As Jill and Elia negotiated, the sales manager approached Beth.

"Beth, would you like to join me for a coffee? You must be exhausted after looking at so much furniture. This will give Jill some time to negotiate with your husband over pricing. He can be a demon when it comes to negotiating. It must be that Northern Italian bloodline."

As Beth and the sales manager walk away, Elia hands Jill a check. Jill, I need it delivered to the house on Monday afternoon, okay? Here is some tip money for the delivery crew as well."

As they drove home, Beth asked Elia what would happen next.

"Just give me until Tuesday to see if my new clients send their retainers," Elia said.

"If they don't?"

144

"Well, it will just be a waiting game I'm afraid."

Beth put her head down. "Elia, nothing goes my way."

"Well, Beth, I am expecting a check and signed contract to be delivered to the house on Monday afternoon by courier. Can you make plans to receive it for me? It's really important."

Beth nodded her head as a few tears fell from her sullen face.

Elia arrived home Monday afternoon after the furniture had been delivered and placed per his plan. As he entered the house Beth stood in the hallway admiring the furniture.

"Elia, come look!"

Beth placed her arm around Elia and walked him into the living room.

"Look Elia, isn't it beautiful? Did I do a good job picking it out and doing the furniture plan?"

"Yes, Beth, you did an excellent job, very sophisticated. I am so proud of you. I hope you are happy."

"Elia, let's just stand here and look at it okay, okay?"

"Sure Beth. How about we go out and celebrate this weekend, make a romantic getaway out of it? We can make reservations at our favorite Italian restaurant at the Culinary, then head out for some dancing, and book a room at a quaint bed and breakfast in Cold Spring."

Beth pushed Elia away, as her facial composure changed from contentment to anger.

"Elia, get your fucking hands off me. What do you think I am? Your whore? You just bought me this furniture to show off and manipulate me. There is something wrong with your head Elia. You do good things just to show off and manipulate me."

"Beth, that is not true. I did this to make you happy because you are my wife, and I love you."

Beth placed her hands over her ears and began to stomp her feet.

"Liar, liar, liar! I never wanted this furniture. You just bought it to show off and to put me down. Liar, liar, liar! I hate you! I hate your fucking arrogant educated guts. I curse you and this fucking house!"

Elia is brought back to the present by Anais' rising voice.

"Elia! Elia! Where did your mind go? So, did you ever go au natural?"

"O sorry Anais. I was just thinking about all the fun we are going to have at this 'textile free' resort. And, to answer your question, I only went au natural once in my own pool skinny dipping with Beth."

It's Friday around noon when they arrive at their home for the weekend, a beach-front ground-floor room facing the western Caribbean. The room has large sliding glass doors that open onto a deck. The view is magnificent. They jettison their clothes as soon as they arrive and put on their smiles and sunscreen.

Lounging on the beach under an umbrella, they sip cocktails and frolic together like children in the warm Caribbean water. They are enjoying another one of their shared bucket-list experiences, being totally comfortable with their public nudity. They make conversation with many of the other guests, who for the most part are experienced nudists.

Around dinner time Elia and Anais return to their room to shower and dress for dinner. Clothing, although minimal, is required in the restaurants. After dinner, when the sun has set, a bon fire is lit on the beach and a Caribbean band takes to the stage to provide cool, island, dance rhythms. Soon Anais and Elia relieve themselves of their textile baggage and are dancing in good form around the bon fire, as partners are exchanged without poaching. Everyone is in a hypnotic state. Then around midnight, Anais and Elia slip away to a private hideaway to make love in the wild. Their passions rage as they lust for one another until the early morning hours when they finally collapse. They are awakened by the first rays of the golden dawn. Lying together, embraced on the beach, they laugh and drag themselves to their room to prepare for another day in the native sun.

Saturday is a repeat performance of the day before, except for time they spend in the sauna, pools, and hot tubs with other guests who are good conversationalists, and all card-carrying nudists. The day also includes nude yoga, massages, and meditation classes.

On Sunday evening Elia sits on the deck writing journal entries.

"Elia, writing anything interesting? I'm sure you have some great notes about the sex we had under the waterfall."

"For sure Anais, so much so I may be running out of blank pages in my journal book."

"So, Elia, what's your take on living the nudist life, existentially speaking of course?"

Elia smiles and says with a bit of a laugh, "Is there any other way to speak but existentially?"

"Go on Elia, I am waiting with baited-breath to hear your views on this."

"Anais, nudists live in a very elevated social structure. Just think, here we are, as we are, without pretention or anything to hide. No business suits to cover our imperfections or to project something greater than what we really are. No corner offices, no business cards with a string of letters after our names to impress. We are here, free of our egos, content with ourselves, we hold no negative opinions or judgments. We are free like children, free of the adult shackles of hierarchy and posturing for power. Just think, we meet all these people and enjoy their company just as they are. We are clueless as to their stations in life. They could be doctors, lawyers, carpenters, civil servants, retired, starving artists – it does not matter, we have accepted them as they are. This is immaculate, it's holy, it rises us above the profane, Anais. Have we ever once seen anyone poach another's partner, or hit, or gawk, or make a stupid sexual remark? We have risen above the profane. I will truly miss this place for I now have a bigger dread of the shallow profane world we will return to tomorrow."

"Well said, Elia. I would have not expected less from your philosophical mind."

"I am beginning to believe that the majority of people maintain a puberty level of sexuality, which is far worse than being puritanical."

"Elia, please explain. I need to hear this one."

"Well, just think of the contradictions and double standards most mature adults hold on sex and nudity, so unlike artists. Just think of the number of married couples we know who have children. Having children confirms they must have had sex and enjoyed each other in the nude. So, they have seen naked bodies, become aroused and had sex."

"Elia, go on. What's the point?"

"For most people nudity is the prerequisite for sex. You have people who find their sexual unions boring or they have no sex at all. They begin to fantasize about sex, and in their frustrations, men and women attend strip clubs to be entertained. They go to see naked bodies they want but can't have. So, they drink and drool over bodies they fantasize about, but do not engage in real lovemaking which is their goal. They leave unsatisfied and frustrated. They actually torture themselves."

"How so Elia?"

"It's like inviting people who have not eaten in days to a buffet and telling them they can look and smell, but not eat. This would be viewed as outright cruel and sick. Yet, people with a puberty-level sexuality will believe they are enjoying themselves while they starve themselves sexually. Just look how properly the guests here conduct themselves. They simply enjoy the experience, no gawking, no sexual innuendos, no poaching, no hitting on someone else's partner. You never see this behavior when at a party with adults who still have a puberty-level maturity about sex and nudity."

"You are right Elia. When we return home people will inquire, 'So how was your romantic getaway?' And they will have no problem accepting the fact it was sexually rewarding. If I told my neighbors I went to a nudist resort, they would view me as a libertine or a whore, even if no sex was involved. Can you imagine how they would behave in an art class with a nude model? Imagine grown adults giggling over a naked body."

"Well said, Anais. That's what separates artists from the profane. They lack an aesthetic in life."

"Now Elia, may I speak to you with candor."

"Please do Anais. What's on your mind?"

"Well Elia, have you given our relationship any thought in terms of where it's going? We've only known each other for about eight weeks, and yet I feel I have known you my entire life. Why, I sometimes believe I know you better than I know Ben. I mean where is this going to lead Elia? I have developed very strong feelings for you. You have changed my views on life and have opened new doors of thinking for me. But what kind of relationship will we have moving forward? I mean, we enjoy each other's company so much and I want to be with you, yet just a few weeks ago we were involved in a ménage-a-trois with Morgan. I am confused Elia. Talk to me. Share your views with me."

"Anais, what are you looking for at this time of your life?

What is it you fear? What is it you need? We will have to ask ourselves these questions and be brutally honest. We must also remember that if we really believe we need each other at this time in our lives, we need to consider if it is out of necessity, love, or fear. And if we do need and love each other, are we really enough for each other? And, what about Ben, the master Svengali?"

"Yes Elia, you are right. We need to do some soul searching to see where we want this relationship to go. I am enjoying it without exception, and we both want each other in our lives, but we need a direction and understanding."

"For sure Anais, the honeymoon will not last long and can easily turn into mediocrity – what we both are running from. We both will need to give this some serious thought."

They make love in their room one last time before they head to the airport. They are happier and wiser, though confused.

The Call

I am home at my loft sketching out themes for my next gallery exhibition, lost in an existential paradise. I am relaxed and reflective, thinking about how well my life has been going since my divorce and my hot relationship with Anais. For the first time in my life, I am beginning to enjoy the fruits of my labors. My phone rings, intruding upon my tranquility. I hesitate, not wanting to be awakened from this pleasant daydream.

"Hello," I say with reservation.

"Hey Elia, it's Rit, you sitting down?"

"Why Rit? What's up?"

"Well Elia, I have some rather bad news for you. I just received a call from Beth's attorney. He informed me that Beth had a mental breakdown and was institutionalized a few days after she signed the divorce papers and the house was placed on the market. He presented the case to the courts. Well, augh..."

"Rit, please go on. Don't hold me in suspense. What's the problem?"

"Well, the judge has reviewed the divorce agreement and feels it may be invalid since Beth signed it in a state of insanity. Beth is being influenced by Sal who sees money in this, not only for Beth, but for himself as well. He believes there is a windfall here and is likely looking to help himself to the booty to extract himself from his delinquent alimony and child support. They are playing hardball! So, technically, from a legal perspective you are still married until we can present your case to the judge. So, Elia, do you existentialists have a term for such a conundrum?"

"Yes Rit, it's called getting fucked without the benefit of an orgasm!"

"Elia, why that is so out of place for a man of your refinement and character."

"Well, Rit, take a look on the bright side. I could have said, fuck you Rit, you're fired, I will retain a real attorney. Ha, ha, ha."

"Well Elia, you're in a precarious position, possibly unwinnable, even with proof of Beth's infidelity. You believe you are divorced and enter a relationship with a beautiful, sexy, hot woman. You are seen with her at ribbon-cutting ceremonies and at all your new design projects throughout the Hudson Valley. With Anais' business contacts all of this is amplified in press releases. Yes Elia, you have received much press which conveys that you are now very successful and making a lot of money. You are an easy target for the courts and public opinion."

I walk over to the window to calm myself with a view of the Hudson River. It is glistening under an early, sunny, winter sky.

"So Rit, do we have a chance?"

"Elia, *fatta la legge, trovoto l' inganno.*[15]"

"Rit, so what's the plan? What should I do?"

"Elia, for one, lay low, no more press releases or filmed ribbon cuttings with Anais at your side. Keep a low profile. Take Anais to places out of town. Speak softly and with caution to all. Assume that not all your old friends are really your friends. Envy breeds traitors and opportunists."

"Rit, should I share this news with Anais?"

"Elia, you moral fool. Don't forget who her ex-husband is.

---

[15] "There is always a loophole."

Even if Anais is not unnerved with the news, if Ben gets wind of this, you will have much to lose. You capiche my friend? Can you trust Anais not to share this with Ben?"

Thy Neighbor's Wife

"Thou shalt not covet thy Neighbor's wife."

I am on my way to pick up Anais for a B.B. King Concert and then to head out for a romantic weekend in New Hope, PA. My mind is racing, I'm confused and concerned about the state of my divorce. Is it binding or will the judge rescind it since Beth signed the papers just a few days before she was admitted to the hospital for her nervous breakdown? My attorney believes the divorce is still binding, though he has warned me about all the press coverage I've had surrounding my recent professional success. I have been seen and photographed at numerous events with Anais at my side. I know the courts will have a field day with this.

"The once moral Elia is now at the center of a sex scandal with an actress whose steamy new movie is to be released in a few months," I say out loud.

My brain virus is spreading through every nerve of my body as I begin to address the uneasy feelings I've had about Ben ever since I first met him at Anais' home. It's strange that he's frequently at the house, even when his daughters are not home. Ben always says he's dropping off checks or gifts for his girls. He's perfectly comfortable in the house, laid out on the couch watching a video, or fixing himself something to eat. Anais is always okay with this, even when Ben greeted me at the front door in his robe last week.

Where has my life taken me? – Amor fati, as Camus wrote.

I pull into the driveway and park next to Ben's Mercedes Benz. Sensing a coming storm or perhaps a moment of truth, I slowly approach the door with a bit of trepidation. Gathering my thoughts, I wonder what is really going on here. I take a deep breath and ring the bell.

Anais answers wearing a thong, standing tall in a pair of stiletto heels. She is completely made-up. She pushes up against me, hugs me tightly, and kisses me passionately with a French kiss.

"Give me a few minutes to throw on my clothes. It won't take me long. I can't wait to see the show. This will be my first B.B. King concert. I can't wait," Anais says as she begins to ascend the open center-hall staircase.

I savor the view, and for a moment my misgivings give way to pure sexual fantasy.

"While I am dressing, just go into the family room and chat with Ben. He is waiting for the girls to arrive to take them to the movies. It's his weekend to have them."

Before Anais reaches the top, I am greeted by Ben.

"Anais is so beautiful. I can watch her all day in her natural state. As you can see, she is not the least bit inhibited," Ben says.

He places his arm around me. "Good to see you again, my friend. You have made such a positive impact on Anais. She never stops talking about you. Why I sometimes feel a bit jealous and intimidated, especially when she shares your sexual exploits with me. Very impressive Elia. Must be that intellectual, existential, artistic charisma."

"Does Anais share our intimate times together with you so candidly?"

"Of course, Elia. As you know there are no secrets held between the bed sheets. Besides, why would you care? It's all good press. And Morgan seems to agree. You lucky man."

I am stunned.

"So, Ben, you don't think it's inappropriate for your ex-wife to parade around naked in her house in front of you?"

"O Elia, may I remind you, I have seen Anais naked for years. You of all people are criticizing Anais for being uninhibited? Ooh Mr. Moralist, do you need to be reminded? 'He who is free of this sin, cast the first stone.' Elia, are you having a memory lapse? Anais and Morgan shared their stories of the three of you escaping for a weekend ménage-a-trois at your loft. You lived every straight man's sexual fantasy. You spent a weekend with two bisexual married women, and it was condoned by their husbands. Why the saddened face Elia, too much pussy got your tongue? O my dear Elia, you are either a hypocrite or a martyr without a cause, or some unappreciative and tormented soul. What have you to say for yourself, humph?"

"*Il troppo stroppia...Beni*[16]," I say. And then, what Ben has said hits me.

"Ben! Just what the fuck are you talking about? Are you telling me you and Anais are married and so is Morgan? Is this one of your Svengali mind-games, Ben?"

"O Elia, if it is, one would think you are the big winner. Congratulations Elia, your stories will make you a legend! Oh, I forgot, Elia the gentleman does not kiss and tell. Ha, ha, of course you don't out of morality and self-respectability. No, no, no, Elia! Maybe you don't kiss and tell because of, now what commandment is it? 'Thou shall not covet thy neighbor's wife.' Well, technically, you didn't covet your neighbor's wife, you fucked two of your neighbors' wives, blind to the fact they were married. Well, poor Elia, maybe you are right. This may be forgivable.

"This is so ironic. Anais tells me how much you lament the possibility your divorce may be rescinded by some technicality

---

[16] "Too much of a good thing can be harmful."

and that you throw stones at yourself like some hapless martyr believing you are an adulterer. Yet, all the while, you are having sex with two married women. What do your fucking moral philosophy books have to say about that? Elia?"

I feel a rage building within and fear I cannot hold my calm demeanor much longer. Ben is making a fool of me with his street smarts. I will not let this consummate manipulator and persuader get the best of me. I rush over to him.

"Elia, stop! I can break you in half. You have no fight in you, do you Elia?"

"Physically speaking, you are right Ben, I afford you no real physical challenge. You should question yourself Ben, does not a strong mind trump a strong back?"

Ben is getting very hot under his collar. "Where is Bronson now?" he shouts.

Elia shakes his head. "Yes Ben, it is true, there appear to be no secrets kept between the sheets of passion."

"Elia! Spare me your poetics, cute intellectualism, and martyr's pity. Elia, the moral existentialist, in light of the bacchanalian lifestyle you have been living over the past few months with Anais, and to a degree with Morgan, I would say your morality is a bit languid, hypocritical, to say the least. O Elia, you pathetic and pious fool. Here you are in an existential tailspin, falling into the abyss of your own fantasies, worrying about the judge rescinding your divorce and that you may now be living the life of an adulterer. Open your fucking eyes to see what your flesh has experienced and savored. I am driven by the desires of the flesh and pure materialism, Elia. I have no thoughts of an eternal morality. I deny the soul and view God as just an obstacle in my path to an epicurean life. Can you deny the sensual pleasures you experienced with Anais and Morgan? Why Elia, you torn and contorted intellectual and moral soul, here you are having an open affair with my wife, which I condone. Then you engage in a ménage-a-trois with Morgan who is bi-sexual and by the way also married, and whose husband allows your dalliance with her without reservation. O Elia, you so much lament, yet your sexual realities have exceeded the fantasies of most men. Why and what do you lament? Will you lie to me and say you have regretted your actions and did not find them pleasurable? Huh, Elia?"

"Ben, I cannot lie. Lying is as much a sin as adultery. I will confess I enjoyed every moment I spent with Anais – not knowing she was married and believing I was divorced at the time. Ben, please give me credit for this. Am I guilty by believing and following the lead of someone who misled me?"

"O Elia, then what about your dallying with Morgan and Anais together? Were you not just like most mortals falling to the temptations, which you repressed under the lighted signpost 'Taboo'?

"Yes Ben, in truth, I enjoyed breaking the taboo, and most of all the sensual delights it rendered me. This only proves I am human. But where you and I differ – I have a conscience."

Responding to Elia's low sarcasm, Ben begins to raise his voice, pushing off the challenge to his character.

"So, Elia, are you obsessed with your divorce 'problem' more from a moralist perspective than a financial one? Why it is quite ironic. You catch your wife in an illicit affair, secure the divorce, then go out and have a grand affair with Anais, all within the public eye, only to find the judge has rendered the divorce invalid since your 'ex' wife signed it in a poor mental state and is now petitioning the courts to have you charged with infidelity. What a mind fuck Elia. But personally, I see no problem with your actions. I am sure Anais has been able to comfort you during this whole ordeal. Why Elia, Anais has told me so often how you two, uhm, three, had such great sex together. O Elia, you lucky dog, even Morgan has endorsed this claim, going on about all this Kama Sutra and Tantric sex you got them into. Well, what do you have to say for yourself? Why, Elia, I am not sure if I admire you or am just outright jealous?"

"Excuse me Ben, I am not one who appreciates flattery."

"Elia, you are an intellectual and a man of letters, yet you confound me with your contradiction of good versus evil. These are not words of static definition – they are dynamic and flexible. Wouldn't you agree Elia? You see sin and irony in your own pleasures when you should be thankful and guilt free. You should rejoice knowing that in a few short months you have lived most men's sexual fantasies. Yet, you lament. Who is throwing stones at you Elia? Why the sad face when you have been having the best sex with such a beautiful woman as Anais? Your moral remorse is a bit insulting to Anais I would think. As a poet, have you forgotten Ovid's words? 'Not by some legal decree did you and she end up in one bed, love is law for you two, armed with legitimate rights. Seeing your loved one again brings words of pleasure and solace; each visit of yours makes it a red-letter day.'

"You see Elia, I am a man of limited morals. I have been cheating on my dedicated and faithful wife from the start of our marriage. And, like yourself, the self-proclaimed moralist you claim to be, after all these years I realized I was denying Anais all of the pleasures I so much enjoyed at her expense. And, being in the entertainment business, I was in a position to bed as many starry-eyed young actresses as my libido could handle. Anais just stopped turning me on. So, we made an arrangement, we agreed that she can go out and have an affair with the intention of finding someone who really turns her on. And, if she found that someone, we would stay married in an open relationship, you know for that old and useless cliché, for the sake of the kids and to secure our financial future. But it is all an illusion. We do it to insincerely fit in with the lost nomadic herd, forever lost in convention and tradition to look respectable. You see Elia, we do have so much in common, wouldn't you agree?

"O Elia, you poor romantic moralist, you seem offended by this, yet you are the one fucking my wife and her lesbian lover, enjoying it without any inhibition. Why what good is having great sex without sharing it with friends? Elia, look at it as an exotic vacation. When you return home do you hide the photographs and not share your adventures with friends? Don't you own bragging rights on the photographs and the stories, Elia? Why, you should feel proud of your sexual antics with Anais, and at times with Morgan when she is not with me!"

"What the fuck are you talking about, Ben? What is going on here? Tell Me Ben. I need answers."

"Elia, you poor moralist bastard. You just want fucking answers when everyone else just wants to get fucked. Here you are in a contested divorce, singing your morality tale, while you are being charged with infidelity by your maybe 'ex' and fucking my wife and her lesbian lover, who just so happens to be in an affair with me. So, who holds the monopoly on morality? Morgan has every right to share her sex stories about you with me! And without reservation. Why are you and Morgan an exclusive? Now Elia, get off your high horse, please. Besides Anais could be hearing this."

"Then why is Anais sharing our sexual encounters with you?"

Ben is very calm. At Elia's expense he is having fun bantering with a *pisan* intellectual.

"So, Elia, don't you always say to Anais there should be no secrets in a relationship? And partners should not hide anything from each other? Correct me Elia, are these not your words?"

"Yes Ben, this is correct."

"Tell me Elia, as a man of morality and restraint, in the heat of passion and desire with Anais and Morgan, if they had whispered in your ear that they are both married and have children, would you have stopped your ménage-a-trois? Tell me Elia!"

"Ben, no more than a levee can hold back a raging sea can I lie to say I would deny the pleasure."

"Well Elia, you know as well as I, life is not a calm sea. The realist navigates his ship around the tempest to reach a safe harbor. The fool is the one who turns a calm sea into a tempest for some philosophical purpose and ideology. The hypocrite is the one lost between ebbs and flows of each tide, exposing his vulnerabilities at low tide while he hides all his indiscretions under high tide. You, Elia, are the moralist who stands upon the stormy sea to calm it, blind to the delights and the bounty of its raging."

"Ben, what are you getting at? What are you trying to tell me?"

"Elia, my friend, you can't mold or design one's emotions or actions like you can sculpt a building. You are quite the romantic Elia, and you can satisfy women. But even a master builder is forced to work within the laws of mathematics and physics. As a great lover of life's aesthetics, the flesh included, you must learn to live within the laws of our frail emotions. Elia, not everyone is a magus who can control his emotions with logic and cold restraint. Where did your high morality and fidelity get you with your wife? Was Beth not enjoying Sal between the sheets as you practiced your morality? Did you believe Beth could uphold such a standard? She loved you more when she was in bed with Sal or getting shit-faced with him at some red-neck bar. Elia, don't you love Beth more today for pushing you out of her life and into the arms of Anais? You are the better and wiser man. Does not Anais excel over Beth in every way? Elia, a moralist is a wise man even when he sins. Infidelity is never time sensitive, and for the most part inevitable when unfulfilled passion and desire are at stake. Anais and I hold firm that infidelity can never be determined by a judge's gavel. It can only be determined by our definition of infidelity itself, both physical and emotional. So how can we believe the legal system can impose or deny us our passions and desires?

"Elia, Anais and I value honesty and harbor no secrets between us. She enjoys your company more then she enjoys mine, as I enjoy my time with Morgan more than I do with Anais. You see, Elia, both Anais and I respect you and are concerned about you. She tells me how you are playing the role of a martyr feeling guilty about your 'infidelity' brought on by a lapse in the legal system. We believe your rationale is silly and misguided. At best, the situation is a human comedy of errors and omissions. Why Elia, you have stronger feelings for Anais than I do. So, we feel to save ourselves from ourselves, we will have an open marriage. You see Elia, while you have been beating yourself senselessly over this alleged infidelity with Anais, you have been oblivious to the fact that you were having an open affair with my wife. Now Elia, see how ironic and absurd life can be? In a way it is quite humorous. So, Elia, whether or not your divorce is legally binding, Anais and I are still married. After years of arguing and growing apart, and not to mention my string of illicit affairs, Anais has remained faithful to me. To be fair to Anais, I agreed to support her while she had an affair of her own and if she found the right man, I agreed we could continue in an open marriage. Nothing will really change, except we will both be happier."

"Ben, I cannot believe I am hearing this. When you decided on this arrangement did you and Anais think of my feelings?"

"O Elia, is your stone façade backed by mushy emotions? Why yes Elia, we are concerned about your emotions, and we both want you to be happy and free to explore your sexuality with the right woman. Are you not a better, wiser, and happier man now that you have found each other?"

Ben pauses for a moment as both men reflect.

"Elia, just think, we have both enjoyed the same women, who I hope enjoyed us equally as well. And those women enjoyed each other. Why do you see yourself as a repentant monk covered in ashes and sack cloth, Elia? Why do you flagellate yourself? Open your eyes Elia, you have lived a reality that most men can only fantasize about. Tell me Elia – you are an intellectual, artist, romantic and a natural lover of women – are you going to deny me the truth that you have penned your last few months of journal entries without glee and satisfaction? Are you going to deny that you are a fortunate man? Elia your harsh self-criticisms are unwarranted. Why do you seek pity like a beggar groveling for stale bread? For heaven's sake Elia! Fuck the courts, the judges and the lawyers! They have no place or right to rule your heart and emotions, let alone your fucking dick!"

"Tragedy by means of legends and emotions, creates a deception in which the deceiver is more honest than the non-deceiver, and the deceived is wiser than the non-deceived."
–Gorgias (Sicilian Rhetorician 5th century BCE)

"Elia, you want my sympathy for setting you up in this Machiavellian game as you lament having been deceived and made a fool of. The reality is you, Elia, with your cerebral thinking, have actually deceived the deceiver at his own game.

Who is the street-smart Svengali now, Elia?" My game plan for Anais was for her to engage in some sexual liberation and freedom as an epicurean and Bacchanalian experiment, free of all emotional attachment. It was intended to be something Anais could easily walk away from after filling her pending middle-age bucket list. I never believed she would fall for you, even with your charm, sophistication, and spirituality. Really, how could she fall for any man but me? O Bravo Elia, you have deceived the deceiver! You have made a fool out of me in front of my own wife, and even Morgan. Yes, Elia, you have transmuted Anais' desire for your flesh to her desire for your soul. Elia, Elia, Elia, the true Gnostic magus.

I am angry and jealous, Elia, and most resentful of your snobby, arrogant and well–heeled Northern-Italian attitude. Who the fuck are you kidding? Your roots are only a few small footsteps north of the Mezzogiorno line. You know, it doesn't bother me that you are physically fucking my wife, and she's enjoying it. But it does bother me that you have seduced her emotionally and spiritually and awakened her soul. When we are alone together, all she talks about is Elia! In her sleep she whispers your cursed name! Elia! Elia! Elia! What kind of a man are you, huh? Fucking is just for the sharing of body fluids."

"My dear Ben, true lovemaking is a marathon, not a 50-yard sprint. It is more about sharing emotions and one's soul. It's not just a sprint to a flaccid dick."

"Elia, Elia, I don't mind giving my wife to you to fuck, I can live with that. But I won't lose her in a competition with another man, especially someone like you. Elia, *Tra moglie e marito non mettere il ditto.*[17]

---

[17] "Do not place a finger between husband and wife."

"Ben, thank you. *Uomo avvisato mezzo salvato*[18]."

"Elia, I have been generous and giving, but remember who I am, where I come from, and who I know."

While Ben and Elia have been talking, their voices angry and rising, Anais has come downstairs, Morgan has entered the house unannounced, and Ben and Anais' daughters have arrived home. They retreat to the kitchen, confused as to what is going on and what to do about it.

"Elia, you are pushing my hot fucking Sicilian temper. Capiche? Huh goomba?"

Ben slams Elia against the wall.

"Hey Elia, what's ya goona do?"

"Ben, I believe you are the one doing the pushing."

Totally out of control and raging like a bull, Ben grabs Elia by the collar and shoves him up against the wall.

"Elia, do you fear me? Do you hate me, Elia? Huh?"

Ben then throws Elia a sucker punch across his face. Elia's head recoils then slouches back.

"Hey Elia, lover boy, you gonna hit me? What's ya going to do? Huh? You gonna hit me back, you fucking medigan?"

"I will only turn my cheek to such violent action."

"Don't test me, Elia."

Ben throws Elia another hard punch across his other cheek. Blood splatters everywhere. Elia is bleeding from his nose and mouth.

"Hey Elia, I just bloodied your other cheek. You ain't got no more cheeks to turn Elia. What do you say Elia?"

"I will pray for more cheeks to turn, Ben."

Elia's composure taunts Ben and he slams him up against the wall. The house shakes violently. Anais, Morgan, and the three

---

[18] "Forewarned is forearmed."

daughters, having heard the conversation, walk in to see what's going on.

"Elia! Elia! Elia! Hit me, dam you hit me. Fuck you Elia, hit me, do something! What are you, a fucking jadrool[19]?"

"Ben, I hold no grievance against you or your house. What will be gained? What will be achieved if I engage this fight? My defense will only be an attack on my pacifist beliefs. Ben, basta, basta[20], you capiche?"

"Elia you must be obatzo[21]."

"No Ben, crazy people don't stand down a fight or hold malice towards the world. Now Ben, enough, enough. I fear no mortal Ben, only humanity's ignorance. I pity you Ben and your foolish macho bravado. Your actions only make you a spoiled and insecure fool in front of Anais, your children, and Morgan. My reserve is my resolve and your unwinding."

Ben begins to calm down.

"Tell me Elia, how do you hold your calm and reserve against someone like Sal who is fucking your wife behind your back? I mean, don't you just want to strike out at him? I mean Elia, what did you say and what did you do to him when he confronted you?"

"I simply shook his hand and said I respect any man who takes away my garbage."

"Elia? Elia? You are obatzo. I am sorry Elia. I am sorry. I let my temper get the better of me. I guess I am jealous after all. Will you ever forgive me, Elia? Are you going to call the police?"

"No hard feelings Ben. I hold no malice or grievance against you. It's a small penance for all the trouble I have brought to this house. No Ben, I am sorry."

---

[19] "Stupid person."
[20] "Slow down, chill out."
[21] "Crazy."

Elia drops his head and looks down at his uncle's ring.

Anais walks over to Elia with a cloth and starts to wipe away the blood.

"Elia you are hurt, looks like a broken bone or two, does it hurt bad?

"No Anais, very little, it's a small price one must pay for happiness."

"Elia, what about the scars and broken nose?"

"Anais, you know how I loathe clichés, but beauty is only skin deep."

As Ben watches, Anais snuggles up to Elia and they embrace. Ben's temper begins to flair and as he storms out of the house, he approaches Elia, looks into his face, gently slaps him on one of his bloodied cheeks and whispers in his ear, "*Scherza coi fanti e lascia stare i santi*[22]." Slamming the door, he gets into his Mercedes and red lines it down the street.

"Elia, what did Ben say?" Anais asks.

Elia just shakes his head and mumbles, "*Il diavolo non e cosi brutto cone si dipinge*[23]."

"What did you say Elia?"

"O nothing, just a mantra of sorts."

"Anais, see where this game has taken us. Instead of painting icons to lead us to heaven, we created an idol to worship that led us to hell. We have become like the mystical snake ouroboros who eats his own tail. We have only one direction now Anais, I must leave you as I love you, for soon our love will expire and turn to hate and we will even forfeit our beautiful memories of each other. Anais, we shared and lived the romantic aesthetic life together and it was played out against the backdrop of our ugly

---

[22] "Serious things are not to be taken lightly."
[23] "The devil is not as ugly as he is portrayed."

and frail humanity."

"Elia, believe me, I never thought my experiment would go this far. I was just looking for someone to satisfy my pent-up sexual desires. I would never have believed when we first met my physical attraction to you would sprout emotional roots that would grow deep within my soul, a soul I have always denied. Elia, after what Ben has done this evening, I feel guilt for the first time deep in my soul. You, Elia, led me to my soul, now I dam it to fucking hell."

"Elia, you are different, an outlier of this wretched fucking twisted humanity. You are lofty, though never above anyone. You see through the darkness. I can't grasp your mind, though I have held your soul. Elia, do you now hate me?"

"No Anais, I can only love you more."

"How Elia? How, after what Ben did to you and his threats? Explain it to me, a spiritual neophyte, please."

"Anais, when we make love, my mind finally goes silent, the intellectual three-ring circus leaves town. There are no more equations in my head, no philosophers to talk to. I become free, like I am in a clear pure river that moves my soul eternally. I have never before experienced this emptiness that fills me with abundance until I made love to you. Anais, my mind is a blessing, wrapped in a curse. So, Anais, how can I hate you for calming my never-sleeping mind? Maybe one day we will both find ourselves seeking to free ourselves from the mad and profane by bathing in the clear water of the mystical river as it purges us of our pains and speaks the language of angels."

Elia goes over to Anais, gives her a big kiss.

"Anais, I have to leave now."

"Elia, where are you going?"

"I need to spend some time with an old friend."

"Elia, is it someone I know?"

"Sure Anais, I introduced you to my friend when we first met. Now let me run."

"Elia, I don't like the sound of this. Are you sure you're okay?"

"I will be fine Anais."

"Elia, Elia, don't go! Will I see you again?"

"For sure Anais, we'll kiss on a distant shore."

Elia exits the house with Anais at his heels.

Elia! Elia! I don't understand! Stop talking to me in your fucking riddles! Elia! Be careful Elia! Ben is out of control. Elia, please! Elia! Augh, fucking existentialists!"

Elia's Paradiso

"That is always how a person acquires courage:
when he fears a greater danger, he always has courage."
–Soren Kierkegaard

I enter my car, start up the engine and dim the dashboard lights. The low idle of the motor envelopes my senses, its rhythm vibrating through me like a sacred mantra. I turn off the radio and cassette player so I can meditate and think of my old friend. That always makes me happy. I am soon lost in one of my cerebral brain dialogs. My mind is on intellectual overload as I visualize myself as the ringleader of my own three-ring academic circus. I need this mental banter to take my mind away from the bad scene I just left at Anais' home.

"Ladies and gentlemen, children of all ages, welcome to Elia's three-ring circus – the greatest show on heaven and earth. Now please join us and give a big round of applause to our first entertainer Dante Alighieri who will perform his Divine Comedy. In the first ring we have the Inferno, in the second ring we have Purgatorio, and in the center ring, Dante himself in Paradiso."

In my frenzied brain virus, I reflect on the four cardinal virtues of Prudence, Justice, Temperance, and Fortitude, then upon the three theological virtues of Faith, Hope, and Charity. I imagine Anais as Dido and my guide in Paradiso who takes me to the spheres of heaven where we stop at Venus, the third sphere for lovers traditionally associated with the Goddess of Love. Like Dante, I believe this is the place for lovers deficient in the virtue of temperance.

"You shall leave everything you love most dearly;
This is the arrow that the bow of exile
Shoots first. You know the bitter taste.

Of other's bread, how salt it is, and know
How hard a path it is for one who goes
Descending and ascending others' stairs."
–Dante

I continue with my self-imposed mental amusement. "Ladies, gentleman, and children draw your eyes to the high-wire trapeze act of Descartes' Metaphysical Dualism as he walks the tightrope that divides the spiritual world from the physical world, never to be bridged."

Well, if Descartes can't bridge this fine line, then I'm not expected to. This gives me some sense of relief from my sexual enigma. But, as I continue my inner dialog, I am confronted by further contradictions.

Descartes' rationalism tells us knowledge is derived through reason from innate ideas. Though Aristotle's empiricism will have us believe knowledge is based on our fallible sense experience. Maybe they are both right, we exist in a dualistic world of conflict between soul and matter – an unsolvable equation and obstacle to transmute our existence into essence. Or is essence just a sporadic placeholder that occurs in our life out of synchronicity?

My mind, now lost within my mental three-ring circus, is broken with sarcasm. I fight to ease my brain hemorrhage. Maybe we live in a world where the words of the great philosophers sound like carnie talk to the profane masses.

I sigh with relief for a moment to break my mental mind games. Then my divorce situation filters back into my mind like a non sequitur. "Shake off this thought with indifference," I mutter to myself.

Tempus omnia medetur[24]

I laugh as I catch myself reciting a cliché. Maybe mortal life is merely another cliché. I am beginning to believe this. How else can we explain our frail human condition?

Were Plato and Aristotle right when they reasoned that the state has primacy over the family and individuals, offering no self-sufficiency for individuals? Or does one find true happiness in accordance with moral virtues sustained over a person's lifetime as defined in Aristotle's Nicomachean Ethics?

I use these questions as taunts. I am such a moral masochist, punishing myself with thoughts of the smallest breaches of my morality. I never believe for a moment they are 'alleged' or even forgivable.

As a moralist and ideologist, I would like to believe in Plato's discourse in *Symposium*, which states that love can lead us to truth. The sad truth is that reality is the experience that teaches us love and lies are the duality of all relationships, leading us to the conclusion that long-term relationships are difficult to sustain without deception. The goal of love is to find our other half. A goal for many that requires lies and believing in lies that one should never have to believe when under the duress of love. It's a hybrid of love, art, and deception interwoven into our twisted psyche that begs the question, "Is falling in love a cruel game we call happiness?"

Stendhal described the process of erotic love as having four phases – admiration, acknowledgement, hope, and delight. It's the latter that is our Achilles heel. Because we are human, we resort to our fallible senses and nourish the delights of our love

---

[24] Time heals all wounds.

by overrating the beauty and character of our paramours.

I am obsessing on what has transpired over the past few months. How will it impact all the players in the future? For better? For worse? Will it leave deep scares of pain, anger, regret, and revenge? Or simply be accepted as life as it is?

I continue to ponder, looking for the 'Why' from a legal, philosophical, moral, spiritual, and existential perspective. I want to find closure, or at least formulate a calculus to solve this emotional equation. Can erotic harmony ever be found by analogy of opposites? I entertain this new Rubik's cube within my head, resigning myself to conclude that in the search for the essence of life only sin can bring unity to the body, mind, and soul simultaneously on the physical plane.

I am rewinding my life journey in slow motion as I stop at random thoughts. I take the liberty to detour at each benchmark to re-live moments with my true friends now long gone.

At the break of day, I finally pull out of my brain virus. I have been driving all night on autopilot. I am on Route 9D, heading north, flanking the Hudson River. As I pass Hudson Park all-night diner, I catch sight of Ben's Mercedes Benz pulling out of the parking lot behind me. I drive on not giving Ben a second thought.

I follow the river as the first rays of a beautiful golden dawn cascades her amber light over its tranquil waters. The river reminds me of an endless strip of movie film pulled through a projector. I downshift and open my window to fix my eyes on the movie of my life in rewind. I feel the cold morning breeze sweep across my face as my car hums in low idle.

I watch as the river takes me back to my youth where along its shore my old friends and loved ones are standing with open arms and smiles. I see them as old, and then young, as the river rewinds my life. They merge into one voice and face. I hear the water sing her sweet Enochian song. It is a bitter-sweet moment as I recall their happy faces and memories, and the pain of knowing they have passed. Yes, it must be so, all the bonhommes have gone home.

I mumble to myself, *"La prima acqua ě quella che bagna.*[25]*"*

---

[25] The first water is what wets.

Anais' Postscript

"Walk me down to the river
Let us dance on its sacred shores
to wade in its low tide
Waiting in hope
for the coming of heaven's door."

I return home late from another failed audition, thanks to Ben and Morgan. I know just how cruel, malicious, and vindictive Ben can be, and now Morgan as well with her solipsism. Ben is and will always be a street bully who has to have his way. I have come to despise Ben, even hate him.

I play back the messages from my answering machine. I finally received the call back from Elia's attorney confirming that Liz will meet me at Elia's loft tomorrow at noon to let me in to retrieve my belongings. I have mixed emotions about this. Are my belongings worth the emotional pain? I pour a glass of Pastis, mix it with water, and gulp it down. This is not like me. I have always loved this French liquor and would sip it with delight. I pour myself another glass to silence the nauseating thought of knowing I am free of Ben, though I am still imprisoned by his money, power, and manipulations. For the first time in my life, I fear him.

I meet Liz at Elia's loft the following day.

"Thank you, Liz, I really appreciate this."

"Well, Anais, don't dally, I have to get back to the office so we can complete Elia's design agreements on time."

"Liz, I understand your anger. May I have a few moments alone to just sit in Elia's loft and mediate for a moment? It means much to me Liz."

Liz opens the door. "I will be waiting in the lobby, don't dally."

The loft is dark except for the light coming through the floor-to-ceiling windows and the skylights Elia had constructed so he could look to the heavens. This was how he juxtaposed his spiritualism into his architecture. It was his way of transmuting his architecture into the spiritual axiom, "The light shines into the darkness, though it comprehends it not."

I remember how after we made passionate love, we would lay naked peering into the heavens as Elia would talk about the eternal journey of the soul and share his Gnostic world with me. I would entertain this, even as an agnostic then, just to not alienate him from his own conversation. I remember once saying to him as we embraced, "Elia the heavens are looking down at us this evening." He would look at me with that Cheshire cat smile, and retort, "Anais as above, so below, as below, so above. No Anais, we are looking down at heaven." As an agnostic I was not able to grasp or appreciate his mystical and spiritual way of life.

I grab my belongings and a few of Elia's writings for memories and safekeeping. I walk to the window and peer out into the Hudson River. I must have lost track of time because the next thing I hear is Liz's knock at the door.

"Anais, we have to go now."

As I leave the loft and lock the door, Liz hands me an envelope. "Elia wanted you to have this, open and read it in private," she says, and then leaves me at the door without saying good-bye.

In my existential break down, I drive over to Karen's, order a Demitasse to go and walk to the river. I sit down at Elia's favorite bench and sip my Demitasse. As I fidget with the local newspaper I had picked up to read, I notice a front-page story about Liz accepting Aprutium Architecture's design award on behalf of Elia for his innovative design of the Behavioral Health wing at Saint Dymphna's Hospital. I pull out my divorce papers. I was planning to serve Ben today. All they need is my signature. I set them down beside me and timidly open Elia's letter. I unfold the note and read:

> *Just follow the river*
> *Listen to its silent call*
> *only one's soul can hear*
> *Its words are mute*
> *Though it calls are never silent*
> *It's eternal.*
>
> *Love,*
> *Elia*

I walk over to the river and gaze into its beauty. The mid-winter light glistens and dances across its mystical waters, reflecting the mountain summits in all their majesty. I feel a tug on my soul, a stirring within, a feeling I have long denied. I no longer feel alone.

I sign the divorce papers and place them neatly on the park bench. I walk closer to the river to hear its magical Enochian call. I take a deep breath, close my eyes, stretch my arms out, and with my head facing up to the glistening mountain summit...I sigh,

"*'O Muroto che pparla*[26]"

The End

---

[26] "The dead person that speaks."

Bibliography

Bonnasse, Pierre, The Magic Language of the Fourth Way, Inner Traditions, Vermont, 2008.

Bush, M.L., What is Love?, London, Verso, 1998.

Camus, Albert, The Stranger, New York, Vintage Books, 1989.

Critchley, Simon, Tragedy, The Greeks, and Us, New York, Pantheon Books, 2019.

Dante, Alighieri, La Vita Nuova, Cambridge, Massachusetts, Harvard University Press, 2010.

Dante, Alighieri, The Divine Comedy, London, Penguin Classics, 2012.

Devillairs, Laurence, The Philosophy Cure, New York, New York, St. Martin's Essentials, 2020.

Editors of goop, The Sex Issue, New York, goop press, 2018.

Fahrun, Mary Grace, Italian Folk Magic, Inner Traditions, Newburyport, MA, 2018.

Goddard, Amy JO, Lesbian Sex Secrets for Men, New York, Plume, 2015.

Greene, Robert, The Art of Seduction, London, Penguin Books, 2001.

Hess, Herman, Siddhartha, New York, New York, New Directions Publishing Corporation, 1951.

Kierkegaard, Soren, The Living Thoughts of Kierkegaard, New York, New York, The New York Review of Books, 1952.

Kierkegaard, Soren, The Sickness unto Death, Penguin Books, London, 2004.

Lavine, T.Z., From Socrates to Sartre, New York, Bantam Books, 1984.

Martin, Clancy, Love and Lies, New York, Farrar, Straus and Giroux, 2015.

Nin, Anais, Delta of Venus, New York, Harcourt, Inc., 1977.

Sartre, Jean-Paul, Existentialism is a Humanism, New Haven, Connecticut, Yale University Press, 2007.

www.ingramcontent.com/pod-product-compliance
Lightning Source LLC
Chambersburg PA
CBHW020330260626
47156CB00004B/1460